One Winner

The Spaniard snapped his hand toward his holster and pulled the .44. Clint's arm moved in a similar flicker of motion as his hand wrapped around his modified Colt.

Both weapons cleared leather at the same time, but Clint was able to aim and pull his trigger before Franco's hammer could drop. The Colt barked once and sent a bullet through Franco's heart. The .44 roared as well but only after a twitching reflex of Franco's finger.

The Spaniard had a surprised look on his face as the fire in his eyes slowly dwindled away . . . and Franco's body landed facedown in the dirt.

DON'T MISS THESE
ALL-ACTION WESTERN SERIES
FROM THE BERKLEY PUBLISHING GROUP

THE GUNSMITH by J. R. Roberts
Clint Adams was a legend among lawmen, outlaws, and ladies. They called him . . . the Gunsmith.

LONGARM by Tabor Evans
The popular long-running series about Deputy U.S. Marshal Long—his life, his loves, his fight for justice.

SLOCUM by Jake Logan
Today's longest-running action Western. John Slocum rides a deadly trail of hot blood and cold steel.

BUSHWHACKERS by B. J. Lanagan
An action-packed series by the creators of Longarm! The rousing adventures of the most brutal gang of cutthroats ever assembled—Quantrill's Raiders.

DIAMONDBACK by Guy Brewer
Dex Yancey is Diamondback, a Southern gentleman turned con man when his brother cheats him out of the family fortune. Ladies love him. Gamblers hate him. But nobody pulls one over on Dex . . .

WILDGUN by Jack Hanson
The blazing adventures of mountain man Will Barlow—from the creators of Longarm!

TEXAS TRACKER by Tom Calhoun
Meet J.T. Law: the most relentless—and dangerous—manhunter in all Texas. Where sheriffs and posses fail, he's the best man to bring in the most vicious outlaws—for a price.

THE GUNSMITH

305

THE SAPPHIRE GUN

J. R. ROBERTS

JOVE BOOKS, NEW YORK

THE BERKLEY PUBLISHING GROUP
Published by the Penguin Group
Penguin Group (USA) Inc.
375 Hudson Street, New York, New York 10014, USA
Penguin Group (Canada), 90 Eglinton Avenue East, Suite 700, Toronto, Ontario M4P 2Y3, Canada
(a division of Pearson Penguin Canada Inc.)
Penguin Books Ltd., 80 Strand, London WC2R 0RL, England
Penguin Group Ireland, 25 St. Stephen's Green, Dublin 2, Ireland (a division of Penguin Books Ltd.)
Penguin Group (Australia), 250 Camberwell Road, Camberwell, Victoria 3124, Australia
(a division of Pearson Australia Group Pty. Ltd.)
Penguin Books India Pvt. Ltd., 11 Community Centre, Panchsheel Park, New Delhi—110 017, India
Penguin Group (NZ), 67 Apollo Drive, Mairangi Bay, Auckland 1311, New Zealand
(a division of Pearson New Zealand Ltd.)
Penguin Books (South Africa) (Pty.) Ltd., 24 Sturdee Avenue, Rosebank, Johannesburg 2196,
South Africa

Penguin Books Ltd., Registered Offices: 80 Strand, London WC2R 0RL, England

This is a work of fiction. Names, characters, places, and incidents either are the product of the author's imagination or are used fictitiously, and any resemblance to actual persons, living or dead, business establishments, events, or locales is entirely coincidental.

THE SAPPHIRE GUN

A Jove Book / published by arrangement with the author

PRINTING HISTORY
Jove edition / May 2007

Copyright © 2007 by Robert J. Randisi.

ISBN: 978-0-515-14301-0

JOVE®
Jove Books are published by The Berkley Publishing Group,
a division of Penguin Group (USA) Inc.,
375 Hudson Street, New York, New York 10014.
JOVE is a registered trademark of Penguin Group (USA) Inc.
The "J" design is a trademark belonging to Penguin Group (USA) Inc.

PRINTED IN THE UNITED STATES OF AMERICA

10 9 8 7 6 5 4 3 2 1

ONE

Johnny Blevin's place wasn't much, but it was comfortable and it was nestled on a fine piece of California property. He was a short ride from the mountains, the ocean, or even Mexico. That made it easy for him to spread word to plenty of friends about the party he meant to throw to celebrate a recent bout of good fortune.

Word of the party spread like wildfire. It spread so quickly, in fact, that the number of people to show up was actually more than double the number of people he'd invited. Johnny took the additional arrivals in stride. Of course, that was easy to do since most of the uninvited guests brought food or drink along with them.

It had been a while since the town had seen a celebration that big. If Johnny had to put up with a few strangers to be the host, then so be it. He was just happy that one guest in particular could make it.

"Someone get a beer for my friend, here!" Johnny shouted as he spotted another new arrival and rushed over to greet him. Johnny was a short man with enough extra weight around his middle to make him look almost perfectly cylindrical. His wiry dark hair and protruding front teeth made him look like an overgrown beaver. At the moment, he looked like a very happy beaver.

Clint smirked and extended a hand to the approaching man. Johnny brushed right past that arm so he could wrap both of his around Clint in a brotherly hug. Clint couldn't help but laugh as he felt himself get nearly lifted off his feet.

"Good to see you, too, Johnny," Clint said. Even though he didn't know most of the people at the party, Clint quickly became uncomfortable as more and more of them stared in his direction. "All right. That's enough."

"Sorry about that," Johnny said. "I'm just glad to see you made it."

"Doesn't look like attendance is much of a problem for this event."

Turning to take in the scene, Johnny nodded as if he were seeing it for the first time.

The property was five acres of mostly flat grassland, bordered on three sides by steep hills. A small, three-room house was in the middle of those three acres and was surrounded by a crooked wooden fence. A wandering trickle of a stream snaked its way behind the house and a small barn was situated nearby.

Just looking at the land by itself, a man could imagine quiet sunrises or even the beginnings of a modest farm. Some pigs could be raised on the property. Maybe a few cows or sheep could be penned in. There was definitely room for horses. Currently, however, there was barely enough room for Johnny and Clint.

Four tables were pushed together to form a single row. On those tables, there was a collection of all the food and drink that had been brought to the party. A few men played loudly upon banjos and guitars, and one of them even beat a rhythm upon an upended bucket. Some folks were dancing. Some were playing games. Here and there, some were fighting. All of them appeared to be having the time of their lives.

"I guess things did get a bit out of hand." Johnny sighed.

"How long has this been going on?" Clint asked. "The letter I got said this was all to start on Sunday. I thought I was going to miss it."

"It did start on Sunday. It's been going steady ever since."

"For three days?" Clint let out a whistle. "You might have a hell of time getting these folks to leave."

Although Johnny winced, he quickly waved it off and said, "To hell with it. I may just hand all of this over to 'em when I leave."

"You're leaving? The last time I checked, you were settling in for good after getting that shipping business up and running."

"And I've still got you to thank for that, Clint," Johnny said as he draped one arm over Clint's shoulder and squeezed. Every breath he let out smelled as if it had been soaked in liquor. "Hey, everyone!" Johnny shouted. "This here's the man who made me the man I am today!"

Although a few of the revelers looked over in Johnny's direction, none of them seemed to be as happy as he was about Clint's arrival. In fact, one of them shouted back, "Who the hell are you two?"

Clint patted Johnny's back. "How about you just point me to something I can eat?"

"Right over this way," Johnny replied. "I'll show you."

"Have you been drinking this whole time? You smell like whiskey."

"Not really. I had a bit, but most of what you smell is what was spilled on me."

The more times Clint was bumped and jostled by drunks, the more he regretted riding in from the coast to put in an appearance at Johnny's shindig. Once he saw all the food on the table, however, his good spirits quickly returned. Grabbing a plate and piling some food onto it, Clint asked, "So what's the reason behind this feast?"

"Didn't I put it in the letter?"

"Nope. All you said was that you wanted me to get here and that you'd tell me about it when I arrived."

Johnny squinted as he thought back to writing the letter he'd sent to Clint. Once that became too difficult, he shook his head and let out a breath. "I thought I wrote it all out." Suddenly, Johnny snapped his fingers. "I remember now! I wrote all of it in the letter I sent to West Texas! Rick Hartman wrote back to me, and I was just barely able to scribble something out and send it to where he thought you'd be. Now that I think about it, I'm even more surprised you made it here at all."

"Jesus, how long have you been planning this affair?"

"Ever since I heard the news."

"What news?"

Johnny straightened up, lifted his chin, and held onto his lapel as if he was posing for a painter. "The news that I'm gonna be so rich that I won't have to work another day in my life."

TWO

At first, Clint thought it was just the liquor in Johnny's system talking. But after studying the other man for a few moments, he saw that Johnny wasn't so unsteady that he should be written off just yet. In fact, Johnny looked more proud than delirious.

"Are you joshing me?" Clint asked.

Johnny shook his head. "Not in the least, my friend."

After filling up the last bit of space on his plate with a helping of beans, Clint led the other man away from the table. "Since I made the ride all the way out here, why don't you tell me about it?"

Johnny acquired a definite strut as he walked next to Clint. They came to a stop at a nearby fence post. The spot wasn't completely free of staggering partygoers, but it was empty enough for Clint to lean against the post and eat his food without the plate getting knocked from his hand.

Letting out the breath that had been puffing out his chest, Johnny said, "There's really not much to tell. You recall that shipping business I started?"

After swallowing the mouthful of food he'd been chewing, Clint said, "I remember the trouble you had in clearing that pass so you could get anything to move through your shipping business."

"Just like I recall nearly getting killed if it wasn't for you stepping in. Did I mention how grateful I am that you stepped up when you did? Otherwise, I wouldn't have ever—"

"You mentioned it, Johnny," Clint interrupted gently. "Several times."

"Well, I wanted to be sure you knew how grateful I was."

"Being invited to this party was all I needed. I haven't had this much food in front of me for a while."

"And as much as I know you can put away more'n your share of food, this ain't the only way I intend on repaying your good deed," Johnny insisted.

Clint tilted his head to one side and squinted as if he were studying the buck-toothed man under a magnifying glass. "What else have you got in store?"

Johnny looked from side to side at the people who were milling about. Even though he was the founder of the feast, nobody else seemed to care too much that Johnny was still there. "Just between you and me, Western Union is buying me out."

"Really?"

Johnny nodded. "Since I was one of the only shippers in these parts who wasn't having trouble getting robbed or making their deliveries, word got around pretty damn quick. Before I knew it, I was doing better business than the post office."

"That's quite a claim."

"But it's one I can back up!" Leaning in, Johnny added, "Especially since I made it my business to be at least five cents cheaper than the post office at every turn."

"I guess that all adds up," Clint chuckled.

"Sure enough! The man from Western Union seemed pretty damned impressed with how I'd done. Seems they've got their fingers in delivering more than just telegrams and they're looking to set up shop around here. I just put a wire in my place . . . you know, to diver . . . uhh . . . differ . . ."

"Diversify?" Clint asked.

Johnny snapped his fingers again and pointed at him. "Diversify! That's it. But it was just talk. Well, the right person heard me talking and the next thing I knew, I was getting an offer from Western Union, themselves."

"Are they going to expand your business or just get you out of the way?"

"To be honest," Johnny said, "I don't give a damn if they want to break my place apart and sell it off for firewood. With what they're paying, I'll let 'em do whatever the hell they want."

"And you're sure the offer is genuine?"

"They already moved in. I got half the money already," Johnny said in a whisper that was almost too low for Clint to hear.

"Please tell me it's not stashed around here."

"Hell no, it isn't. It's safe and sound in a bank where it belongs. I've got some investment plans that might just keep me going for a good, long time. If not, there'll be enough left over for me to start up another business."

Clint used a rumpled napkin to wipe the gravy from his mouth. "That's great news."

"Of course," Johnny continued, "there's still the matter of getting the rest of the money to the bank."

"Sounds like you've already done the job once."

Wincing, Johnny said, "Yeah, but there were some people watching me a little too close. They even followed me a part of the ways back here. I was thinking, since you were heading back soon anyways, that you might ride along with me."

"When were you heading out?"

"I get the second half of the payment the day after tomorrow, but I could leave whenever it suited you."

"Are you expecting this to be as treacherous as clearing out that route from New Mexico?" Clint asked sternly.

"Not hardly! As far as I know, nobody even knows about what I'm hauling or how much money will be with me." After saying that last part, Johnny winced as if he could take it back. At the very least, he wished he would have said it a little quieter.

Clint was thinking along those same lines, but saw that most of the folks at the party still seemed oblivious as to who Johnny even was. "Where's this bank of yours?" Clint asked.

"On the coast no more than a few days' ride from here."

"You're a lucky man, Johnny."

"Why's that?"

"I just happened to be headed in that direction anyway."

For a few seconds, Johnny took the stern look on Clint's face seriously. Then, he cracked a smile and patted Clint on the shoulder. "You almost had me! I was worried you'd tell me to shove my offer where the sun don't shine."

"Now, why would I do that? Especially when you're going to pay me so handsomely for the job."

Johnny kept on laughing, but quickly stopped himself. "Oh, of course I was gonna pay you. I wouldn't ask you to go through all this trouble for free. What sort of wage were you thinking about?"

Having spotted a blonde dancing in a group not too far away, Clint kept his eyes on her as he handed his empty plate to Johnny. "I'm sure we'll work something out just like before."

Johnny let out a breath and took the plate from him. "Yeah! Just like before! I'll even double that! What would you think of that?"

But Clint wasn't paying too much attention to what Johnny was saying. All he'd needed to do was walk halfway over to where the dancing was being done and the blonde walked the rest of the way to meet him. She smiled widely and held her arms open for Clint. When he stepped forward, Clint felt those arms wrap around him tightly and the blonde's body writhing against him.

"My name's Clint."

"I'm Victoria. Who was that you were talking to?"

"I don't know," Clint joked, "but he sure throws a hell of a party."

THREE

The music rose to a frantic level, and the makeshift band played like they were putting on a show for the President. As if following Clint's lead, many more of the people there made their way to the dance, picked out a partner, and kicked up their heels. Two of these dancers were dressed slightly better than the others and slowly moved away from the band so they could hear each other speak.

One half of this couple was a tall man with well-groomed hair, a thin mustache, and skin that was the color of richly tanned leather. His features were sharp, and his eyes burned like two pieces of coal in their sockets. He held onto his partner as if she was the last woman on earth, and he looked directly into her eyes as their bodies moved together.

The woman had long, flowing hair that was dark with the occasional streak of gold. Her skin wasn't as dark as the man's, but was closer to the color of cinnamon. Her body was tight and trim, but still managed to fill out her dark skirt and white blouse nicely.

"You're looking at that man like you know him," the woman said.

"That's because I do know him, Rosa," he replied with a subtle Castilian accent.

"Does he know you?"

"Possibly. I doubt I should bother introducing myself, however. If anything, Mr. Adams would only know me by reputation."

Allowing herself to be swept into a broad circle, Rosa leaned back and let her hair sway behind her. The man leading their dance moved like a bullfighter and made no effort to hide the fact that his dancing had come from classical training.

Even though his face never pointed away from Rosa's, the Spanish man's eyes darted to remain fixed upon Clint whenever possible. He watched as the blonde pressed herself against Clint, and then he turned away when Clint spun around to face his direction.

"Have you introduced yourself to our host?" he asked.

"You know I haven't, Franco."

"Perhaps it is time."

Snapping her head upright so she could stare him down as the music built to a climax, she said, "I am following your lead."

Franco laughed at the banter, wrapped her up in one arm, and then snapped her outward like a whipping extension of his own hand. Rosa twirled while smiling and bouncing off one dancer after another. Within the chaos of the party, she didn't stand out too much, and a few other women twirled even faster as if to outdo her.

Once he saw Rosa separate from the larger group and make her way to Johnny, Franco selected another woman from the crowd and took her in his arms. She was a tall, skinny woman with hair that looked like burnt straw. Her face wasn't quite what someone would consider beautiful, but the smile that showed up there made her a lot more attractive.

"Hey!" the man who'd been dancing with the brown-haired woman shouted. "That's my wife!"

Keeping her eyes on Franco and her hands on the Spaniard's broad shoulders, she replied, "Shut up, Walter. I'll be back in a minute."

As Franco danced, he kept his eyes and hands glued onto his new partner. Actually, his eyes left her every so often to check on Rosa's progress with Johnny. His hands, however, remained attached to her wriggling hips.

Midway through the next song, Rosa tossed her hair over her shoulder and turned to walk back toward the dancers. Franco spotted her immediately and launched himself into a flurry of skillfully moving feet and gyrating hips.

The brown-haired woman did her best to keep up, but mainly watched Franco appreciatively. Just as her husband had decided he'd had enough, she felt Franco pull her in and then spin her away as he'd done to Rosa not long ago. She bumped against her husband, who quickly moved her behind him.

Franco bowed slightly and touched his forehead in a friendly salute. "You are a very lucky man, señor."

"Yeah," the husband grunted. "I know I am."

Between the Spaniard's warm smile and his willingness to step away, the husband didn't have much of a reason to complain. His wife was still worked up, so she quickly pulled him into a bad impression of Franco's dance steps.

Rosa wove through the crowd and slipped into Franco's arms. "He will be leaving soon," she reported.

"Will Adams be going with him?"

"I don't think he's going alone."

"I see," Franco replied.

"Will you kill both of them?"

Franco held her close and rubbed his hips against hers. "I have not decided yet."

FOUR

The party didn't even break its stride when the sun went down. If anything, it picked up an even better stride after the last of the sun's rays had disappeared from the sky. The men who'd been playing instruments all day gave up their spots to another group who picked up various items from nearby and did their best to make music with them. Even though the music wasn't much more than a semi-rhythmic beating of pots, pans, buckets, and chair legs, the crowd was too drunk to notice.

Couples still danced. Drunks still kept drinking. The food disappeared from the tables as if devoured by a swarm of locusts. And more than a few of the people in attendance paired off to disappear to a place with a bit more privacy.

Clint and Victoria were two of those people. The privacy they found was in the back of Johnny's barn. Inside the drafty structure, most of the sounds from the party were blotted out. Replacing that noise were the sounds that came from a few horses and one cow that Johnny had locked up for the event.

Leading Victoria to an empty stall, Clint kicked open the short gate and backed inside.

"You sure there's nothing else in there?" she asked.

Clint kept backing up until his ankle bumped against a stack of hay. "I'm not certain, but there's one way to find out." With that, he toppled onto the hay and pulled Victoria right along with him.

She let out a surprised squeal, but didn't struggle in the least. In fact, she twisted her body to make sure she landed directly on top of Clint. Both of them landed better than if they'd dropped onto a bed. There was more than enough hay on the floor to wrap around them while also cushioning them from the wooden boards beneath it all.

Victoria wore a plain blouse that laced up the front. Those laces had become plenty loose while she and Clint had made their way to the barn. Now she wasn't even able to keep her blouse shut as she twisted and settled on top of him. Clint's fingers slipped beneath the laces to pull them completely out of place.

Although she put a somewhat appalled expression on her face, Victoria only looked down to watch as Clint eased her shirt open. "Why, if I didn't know any better, I'd swear you were trying to take advantage of me."

"You do know better," Clint replied. "You know damn well I'm trying to get you out of these clothes."

"I guess I do. You're doing a fine job of it, too. Here," Victoria said, "let me help you a bit."

Straightening up, she pulled open her blouse and let it fall off of her. She arched her back and used both hands to fix her hair, which was mostly a way to give Clint a good view of her full breasts. They bounced and swayed with the motions of her body. Her large pink nipples grew harder as Clint reached up to take hold of them.

At first, he cupped her breasts and massaged them. Then, he positioned her nipples between his fingers so he could rub them until they were fully erect. Soon, Victoria was leaning forward and situating herself so she was straddling his hips.

"You must think I'm a dirty girl, letting you do this to me," she whispered.

Clint kept one hand on her breast and let the other one wander along her side before rubbing her thigh. "Something tells me you'd like it if I thought that."

She smiled, reached down to loosen Clint's jeans, and nodded. "Maybe just a little."

"Only a little?" Clint asked as he gathered her skirt around her waist and reached between her legs to rub the warm, wet lips he found there.

Gasping as Clint's fingers touched the right spot, Victoria freed Clint's penis and guided it into her waiting pussy. "All right," she whispered as she put him inside and lowered herself onto him, "maybe more than just a little."

Once he was all the way inside of her, Clint lifted his hips and pushed in just a bit more. He was just able to grab her by the hips as she let out a gasp of pleasure and closed her eyes tightly. The more Clint moved, the deeper he and Victoria sunk into the pile of hay. Before long, it was closing in around them as if it meant to swallow them whole.

It took a bit of doing, but Victoria was finally able to gain a bit of footing. Her knees dropped down on either side of Clint, but she supported herself by placing both hands flat upon his chest. Even though she could stay on top of him, she started to wobble the moment she let her instincts take over and tried to ride him in earnest.

Feeling the first pangs of frustration just as much as she did, Clint grabbed hold of her and tossed her onto her back. Victoria landed with a sigh and opened her legs wide to receive him. When she felt Clint's hands move along the silky smooth skin of her inner thigh, she stretched back and savored the feel of his touch.

The downy hair between Victoria's legs was just as blond as the hair on her head. Clint let his fingers drift through that hair for a moment before he found the sensitive nub of skin that made her squirm when he touched it.

"Oh God," she sighed. "Don't make me wait any longer."

Clint positioned himself at the right spot and moved his hips forward so his rigid cock slipped straight into her. Victoria was so wet that he glided in easily. And every time Clint thrust forward, she was even wetter when he pulled back.

Victoria reached out with both hands to grab hold of whatever she could. All she was able to get ahold of was hay, and she kept clawing through the coarse strands until her fingertips scraped against the floor. All the while, Clint kept rocking on top of her. Outside, another makeshift band started to play a drunken song.

"You were sure right about one thing," Victoria said as Clint buried himself inside of her. "This is one hell of a party."

Clint pumped his hips forward until he could feel that soft, blond hair tickle his leg. One more thrust like that, and Victoria moaned as if she meant to accompany the band.

FIVE

It was well after sunrise before Clint woke up and got to his feet. He wasn't in the bale of hay, but he still had plenty of pieces of straw stuck in some uncomfortable places. Victoria was somewhere, but she'd come and gone a few times throughout the night. Clint didn't have any trouble spotting Johnny. He was the one loading a wagon not far from the barn.

"You're up earlier than I expected," Johnny said once he spotted Clint.

"Actually, I was thinking that I slept later than usual."

"Then I guess I'm just getting used to the habits I've picked up in the last few days of debauchery. The closer it gets for me to leave, the more anxious I get to start moving."

"Then why wait?" Clint asked.

The question was simple, but struck Johnny hard enough to make him stop what he was doing and stare into space. He blinked a few times, shrugged, and replied, "I guess there's no reason."

"That is, unless you had a schedule to keep regarding your payment."

"I was told to pick up the money when I had a chance in

the next few days. The rest was just me guessing how long
I should wait for you to arrive."

Clint held out his arms and smiled. "I'm here."

"And you don't mind lending me a hand? It might get
rough if the wrong people find out what I'm carrying."

"And it'll get even rougher if you stand around an-
nouncing it."

Johnny laughed and looked around like a kid who was
trying to sneak out of his house. Apart from himself, Clint,
and the horses, there wasn't another living thing in sight
that wasn't passed out drunk or fast asleep.

"I wouldn't mind getting out of here," Johnny admitted.
"A man can only take so much of this kind of thing."

Even though Clint hadn't quite reached his limit just
yet, he nodded and turned his back to the remaining
women to which he had yet to introduce himself. "What
are you going to do about these folks? Should I start roust-
ing them from their sleep?"

Johnny tossed a passing glance at his little house and
waved it off dismissively. "Nah. Let 'em have the place.
Anything of value has already been broken or loaded onto
this wagon. The property's due to be sold in a month, and
it's only a matter of time before one of these fools burns
the house down. If anyone can get some use of it until
then . . . God bless 'em."

Clint laughed and said, "It must be nice to have a bit of
extra money."

"It sure is, my friend. It sure as hell is."

Eclipse was tied off near a trough closer to the fence
surrounding Johnny's property. Hearing all the commotion
when he'd arrived, Clint figured that would be better than
putting the Darley Arabian where he would be a tempting
target for a drunken horse thief.

As he started to untie the reins, Clint realized the reins
were already untied. He also realized one of his saddlebags

was missing. While looking around for the bag, Clint spotted a figure laying not too far away.

The man was on his side with every one of his limbs pointing in a different direction. He was breathing, but that simple action seemed to cause him a bit of pain. Every inhale was accompanied by a pronounced wheeze, and every exhale was shaky.

Clint bent to examine the man and found a large, dirty imprint on the man's side which was in a peculiarly familiar shape. The man's hand was still clutching Clint's missing saddlebag.

"Looks like you can take care of yourself, huh, boy?" Clint said as he retrieved the bag from the man who'd attempted to steal it. Upon closer examination, Clint could easily spot the shape of Eclipse's shoeprint pounded into the man's side. "I won't even worry about waking this fellow up. I'd say the poor bastard paid his dues in full."

Eclipse stayed in his spot, calmly watching as Clint made sure everything was cinched in its place and ready to go. Once he felt Clint climb into the saddle, Eclipse looked up and shook some of the dust from his mane.

"There's that beauty of a horse," Johnny said. "You sure you don't want to sell him to me? We could make a bundle putting him out to stud."

"Like I said the last time you offered," Clint said as he patted Eclipse's neck, "no deal."

"Can't blame me for trying." In the time that had passed since Clint had gone to get Eclipse, Johnny seemed to have turned into a new man. His smile was brighter. His eyes were wide and alert. He even sat up straighter in his seat and held onto the reins, anxiously waiting to give them a snap.

"Hey," one of the bleary-eyed partygoers shouted from his spot on the ground. "You goin' to get more food?"

"You folks are on your own," Johnny replied. "But thanks for coming out to celebrate with me."

"So . . . no more food?"

Johnny snapped the reins and said, "Not unless you fetch it your own damn selves."

The wagon rattled and shook as it lurched into motion. Although the vehicle wasn't too old and was in fine repair, it was loaded down with just a bit more weight than it was designed to carry. It didn't take long for the wheels to get rolling and the two horses pulling the wagon to find their stride.

Clint rode alongside the wagon and nodded toward the house behind them as he asked, "So you're really not coming back?"

"No need to," Johnny said happily. "I feel a little bad that you didn't get to enjoy more of the party."

"I enjoyed myself plenty."

Johnny smirked. "I'll just bet you did. Victoria looked like quite a party, herself."

"She was."

Both men swapped a few jokes and laughed more than the punch lines deserved. After they'd crested a hill at the edge of his property, Johnny produced a canteen full of lukewarm coffee and handed it over to Clint.

Compared to the swill that had passed for beer the night before, that tepid coffee was good enough to make Clint's morning even brighter.

SIX

The house was full of bodies in various states of undress and unconsciousness. Standing among the sounds of snores and the stench of stale liquor, Franco buttoned up his shirt and watched the wagon through the window. Behind him, Rosa stood up and stretched her naked body like a cat lounging in the warm sun's rays.

"They're leaving," Franco said.

Rosa stepped up to the window, apparently unmindful that she still hadn't a stitch of clothes to cover her. "Maybe they're coming back. I thought he would be here for at least another day."

"Apparently not."

"Should we get ready to leave, as well?"

Franco took hold of her by the hips and pushed her back against the wall. The others in the room with them were passed out or sleeping, but he pulled down his pants and lifted her off the floor as if he wouldn't have cared if he were performing in front of a paying audience.

Within moments after Rosa's legs wrapped around him, Franco slid into her and thrust his hips forward. The flimsy wall shook a bit as her bare bottom slammed against it.

Keeping one arm wrapped tightly around Franco's neck, Rosa reached out to steady herself with the other.

A few of the people in the room were stirring, but that was mostly so they could shift to a better position and fall back asleep. If any of them bothered to open their eyes, they would have seen Franco cup Rosa's tight buttocks in both hands so he could pump into her even harder.

Once Rosa started wriggling her hips along with Franco's rhythm, both of them felt the first stirrings of an orgasm building up in their bodies. The feeling spiked quickly for both of them. As Franco tightened his grip in the start of his climax, Rosa ground herself against him just right so she could follow suit right along with him.

They let out a few prolonged sighs and then Franco pumped his hips once more for good measure. His muscles relaxed, and he backed up to allow her to lower her legs and support herself on her own two feet once more. She placed her hands on his shoulders and leaned up to plant a long kiss on Franco's lips.

"I wish we had time for more," she purred.

Franco responded to the promise in her voice and grabbed her little backside once more. It took some effort, but he just barely managed to step back and pull his pants up so he could buckle them in place. "Later, perhaps," he said.

Neither of them said another word as they gathered up their few belongings and left the house. Even as she stepped outside, Rosa had only managed to get herself halfway dressed. She'd pulled on a skirt, which was all she had to cover her below the waist. Her blouse hung open apart from the bottom two buttons that had been hastily shoved into place. The wind whipped around her, causing her breasts to be exposed and her nipples to grow hard in the chill morning air.

"I'll get the horses," Franco said. "You cover yourself and get ready to ride. I wouldn't want you to bruise anything important."

After taking one more look at her, Franco turned and headed for the barn. Rather than go inside, he walked around the old building to where over a dozen horses had been tied. He picked his and Rosa's out from the animals and led them back to where she was waiting.

"Them's are mine," a man with a grimy face said as he staggered toward Franco.

"Go back to sleep."

Taking another few steps forward, the man raised his voice and spoke so that Franco could fully experience the acrid horror of his whiskey-tainted breath. "I said them's are my horses."

Franco climbed into his saddle, gathered up some slack in his reins, and effortlessly looped the leather straps around the drunk's neck. With one quick snap of his arm, he cinched the reins in tighter and lifted the drunk off his feet as he rode around the barn. Franco grinned to Rosa as he came to a stop next to her. The drunk's heels were just able to scrape against the ground.

"I told you there were a few horse thieves here waiting to take their pick," Franco said.

Rosa's blouse was buttoned, and she was in the process of straightening her skirt after putting on some proper underthings. She studied the drunk's face as it turned to a deeper shade of red. "Wasn't there also another one?"

"I thought so, but I haven't seen him for a while. He disappeared after wandering out past the fence line. Last I saw of him, he was stealing saddlebags."

"What are you going to do with him?"

"Take him with us," Franco said. "At least for a little while. I'd hate to have him stir up any commotion."

Rosa looked around as if expecting some commotion to find them right then and there. Instead, she could only hear a few muffled voices stirring near the house and the occasional gurgle that managed to escape from the choking drunk hanging at Franco's side. Knowing better than to question Franco just then, Rosa climbed onto her horse's back and got herself situated.

"Will you be able to catch those other two?" she asked.

"They haven't been gone that long," Franco replied. "And that wagon won't be moving too quickly."

Rosa snapped her reins and got her horse moving. She rode a little bit ahead of Franco, just to make sure they weren't going to run into any unexpected company on the way out. Franco caught up to her before too long and then he steered off the trail.

Once he'd ridden into a patch of trees, Franco pressed his free hand down on top of the drunk's head and gave his reins a vicious pull. The drunk's neck snapped and his head lolled forward. Franco loosened the reins and allowed the drunk to fall into a heap on the ground.

Rosa looked at him and asked, "Are you sure he is dead?"

Rather than draw the gun from his holster, Franco pulled back on his reins and brought his horse up onto its hind legs. When the animal dropped down again, its hooves pounded the drunk into the dirt. "I am now," he replied. "Come on. Let's catch up to our friend before he and Adams think we forgot about them."

SEVEN

It had been a while since Clint had talked so long with Johnny Blevin. While riding at a leisurely pace, the two men caught up on old times through one story after another. Johnny had always been a funny guy and rarely made a point without doing so in an entertaining way. In fact, Clint would have been amazed at the party from the night before if it hadn't been thrown by Johnny Blevin.

Johnny was just the sort of fellow to throw caution to the wind, put something into motion, and then allow it to spiral so completely out of his control. Because of that, Clint also wasn't too surprised to find out that Johnny had stumbled into such a big amount of money. It took a certain portion of wildness in a man's head for him to put himself into such potentially profitable situations.

Then again, that same amount of wildness was also good at getting a man into a whole mess of trouble. Knowing that more than well enough, Clint figured he would be there to make sure this particular instance didn't spiral too far out of control.

As the day wore on, Clint figured they could have gotten to where they were headed before nightfall if they'd ridden harder from the start. But, since this was Johnny's

show and he didn't seem to be in too much of a hurry, Clint
decided not to get himself worked up about it either. He
just kept his eyes open and enjoyed the ride.

While Johnny was stringing together one story or another, Clint let his eyes wander all around him to look for
any sign that they were being followed. A lot of that came
from instinct and not from the fact that he was there to
keep an eye on Johnny's safety. Sometimes, Clint felt like
he was being followed more often than not. At the very
least, being a bit wary of the matter could never do a man
like him any harm.

They made camp before the sun had fully dipped below
the horizon, and Clint was still convinced they were free of
any unwanted guests. Just to be certain, however, he remained in his saddle after Johnny had climbed down from
the wagon to stretch his legs.

"What's the matter?" Johnny asked. "You don't like this
spot?"

"The spot's fine. I'm just going to circle for a bit and see
if any of those shady characters from your party decided to
chase after us."

Johnny laughed and rubbed the back of his neck. "You
must think an awful lot of yourself if you figure Victoria
would come all this way just to get another poke from the
Gunsmith."

"You might be amazed how far they'll travel for that,
Johnny," Clint shouted over his back.

Johnny's laughter could be heard for quite a while after
Clint rode away from the wagon. Even though he was
laughing along with him, Clint kept his eyes focused on his
surroundings and his ears alert for anything other than
Johnny's voice.

Clint rode out close to sixty yards from the wagon and
made a slow circle from there. Midway through his second
revolution, he brought Eclipse around to face the opposite
direction and retraced his own steps. As far as he could tell,

there wasn't anyone else close enough to pose any sort of trouble.

By the time Clint rode back to camp, Johnny was building a fire.

Franco stood with his back against a tree. Behind him, the two horses were grazing quietly. When he heard the rustle of footsteps, Franco turned just in time to see Rosa walk up a slope on her way back from a river that trickled nearby.

She wore a loose-fitting slip that clung to her wet skin nicely. Wringing out her hair, she sat down and asked, "Did you catch sight of them yet?"

"No."

"Will you be going to make sure they're camped?"

"They haven't moved any further. There's a flat stretch of trail that goes for miles up ahead and they're not on it. That means they've made camp."

"Can you be certain?"

Franco pushed off from the tree and turned around to face her. His hands moved along the smooth leather holster around his waist until one palm came to rest on the grip of his pistol. In a quick, fluid motion, he drew the gun and pointed it at her.

The pistol was a nickel-plated .44 with enough engraving on the barrel to be considered a work of art. There was no sight on top of the barrel and a guard around the trigger that was specially crafted to be narrower and sleeker than its original mold.

Rosa didn't flinch, but instead looked over the gun as if it wasn't even there. "I just don't want you to miss your shot."

The pistol was turned away from her with a fancy spin that twirled the gun around Franco's finger. As the pistol spun, a small gem embedded in its handle caught some of the light to resemble one of the stars twinkling overhead.

After depositing the gun back into its holster, Franco

reached for a rifle that had also been leaning against a tree. "I won't miss my shot," he said confidently.

Rosa crawled over to him and came to a stop so she was kneeling at his feet. She reached up to stroke his crotch with both hands and said, "I bet you could even hit them from here."

"With you making my aim so sharp," Franco replied, "I just might be able to, at that."

"Sounds like we have all night."

"And a generous part of the morning. Since we know where they're going, we can let them get their business done before worrying about catching up to them."

She smiled and began unbuttoning his pants. She seemed more than a little surprised when she felt Franco turn and walk away.

"Not now," he said. "Wait until we're closer to the shot."

After that, Franco sat and disassembled his rifle to make sure every piece was oiled and in its place. Rosa put together a small meal before curling up to sleep by herself.

EIGHT

The Western Union office was a modest building attached to a train station situated on a flat section of green land. It looked more like a house than a place of business simply because it was so new that it hadn't yet had a chance to fall into disrepair. There were colorful curtains in the windows and flowers planted along the walkways.

Since Clint and Johnny had arrived, three trains had come and gone. According to the schedule tacked to the wall, all three of them were right on time.

"You sure you want to sell now?" a portly man in an expensive suit asked.

Johnny froze with pen in hand and looked up. "Why do you ask?"

The second man wearing a suit was younger and sported a dark brown goatee. A dark hat covered a scalp that had little more than short stubble growing out of it. "Sometimes folks change their mind at the last moment, or even not long after they close the deal," the younger man said. "It turns into a costly mess as everyone's dragged through the courts, so we prefer to ask right up front."

Letting out a laugh and shifting his eyes back to the papers, Johnny said, "Not me, Mr. Galloway. Your offer's more than fair and I'm willing to abide by it. You've got nothing but my best wishes."

"That's good to hear."

"Yes, indeed," the portly man chimed in. "Very good to hear. Is there any particular way you'd like the second half of your payment?"

"Pardon?"

"Some prefer gold. Others prefer cash. Small bills. Large bills. It's up to you."

Johnny glanced over to Clint, who mouthed one word slowly enough for it to be unmistakable.

"I guess I'll take it in gold," Johnny said with some surprise.

The portly man smirked and nodded. "A wise decision. I hear there are some very good deals to be had not too far south from here." After that, he disappeared into a back room.

"So," Galloway said as he reached into his pocket and removed a cigar, "who's your partner?"

"This is . . ."

When Johnny trailed off, Clint leaned forward and extended his hand. "Clint Adams. Nice to meet you."

Galloway raised his eyebrows and nodded slowly as he struck a match against the wall. "I've heard that name before." By the time he lit his cigar, Galloway was nodding again. "You're a gunfighter, aren't you?"

"Depends on who you ask, I guess. I prefer to think of myself as a man with many interests."

"Fair enough."

The portly man came back from the next room carrying a medium-sized wooden box. The box was slightly larger than one used to hold cigars, and it obviously took a lot more effort to carry it. "Have a look for yourself and see if this is to your satisfaction."

Johnny's eyes were wide, and he leaned forward as if he

was examining an exhibit in a museum. "That looks really good to me."

"Mind if we take it out of there?" Clint asked.

"Be my guest."

Although Clint didn't empty the box completely, he made sure that the gold bars on the bottom of the box were identical to the ones on top. He then closed it up and said, "Looks good to me. I've just never seen so much neatly cut gold before."

"It never hurts to be careful," Galloway said. "No need to explain."

"The other two boxes are in the next room," the portly man explained. "You can examine those, too, if you like."

Seeing that Johnny was about to bust with joy, Clint stepped in on his behalf. "I'll give them a quick look-see and I'll load them onto our wagon if you don't mind."

The portly man chuckled and wiped his brow. "Not at all, sir. It would save me the trouble of lifting them."

Johnny had to sign another ream of papers to verify the deal was made, he'd received the gold, and all the other legal nonsense was resolved. From there, he stood up and tipped his hat. "It's been a pleasure doing business with you men."

"Likewise," the portly man replied.

Galloway shook Johnny's hand, but didn't bother taking the cigar from his mouth to speak.

Once outside, Johnny climbed onto his wagon and started tugging at the edge of the tarp.

"They're under the seat," Clint said as he walked around the wagon.

Johnny hopped up and bent to reach under the wagon's seat. When his hand bumped against the heavy boxes, he smiled and let out a relieved sigh. Just as he was going to say something, he was stopped by a shake of Clint's head as he climbed onto Eclipse's back.

Johnny's bank was due south from the station, and neither man said anything until the quaint buildings were well behind them. Even then, Johnny seemed a bit reluctant to open his mouth.

"I wasn't sure if you wanted me to say who you were."

"Why not?" Clint asked.

"You know, after all the . . . things you've done."

"Do you think I have a price on my head?"

"No! I mean, you must have angered plenty of men along the way. Last time we rode together, you didn't exactly advertise who you were."

Since Johnny had sweat enough, Clint let him off the hook. "I appreciate the concern, but this is one of those times where it may do some good for folks to know I'm riding with you. If that carries any weight, it might make them think twice about coming after you. If not, it didn't do any harm."

"And . . . what if . . . someone finds out who wants to come after you?"

"Then they would have caught sight of me sooner or later anyway."

Johnny thought about that for a moment and shrugged. Whether it all made sense or not, it seemed to be enough to put his mind at ease for the moment. "You think those two were dealing straight with me?"

"They weren't lying about the price of gold being good right now. I heard about that on my way up here. Also, they didn't try to shortchange you at all. I've got to admit, you're getting more than I thought you would for that business of yours."

"I owned the land, too. Plus, I signed over the name so my usual shippers would know they were still in good hands."

"Those contacts could have been worth a hell of a lot, and you don't have any legal right to them anymore," Clint warned.

Johnny waved his hand as if he were swatting a fly. "They can have 'em. I plan on living simple and only working when I damn well please from here on out."

"Yeah? Well how about we worry about getting to where we need to go before planning out your future."

Johnny looked over with a worried face. "You think someone might be after us?"

"I'm just a firm believer in that old saying about counting your chickens before they hatch."

"I guess that ain't never too good of an idea."

"Nope," Clint said. "It never is."

NINE

The sun blazed overhead with a brilliant, unforgiving light. All things considered, Clint had figured it would be a lot hotter than it was. But the breeze took some of the edge off of what could have been a scorching day, making the ride that much more pleasant.

As the ride wore on, Johnny became more and more aware that he was sitting on a good portion of his hopes and dreams for his retirement. His eyes twitched nervously at every sound. Considering the creaks and groans of the wagon, its wheels, and the horses pulling it, that was a whole lot of twitching.

Clint knew better than to try and keep watch on everything around him. This section of California seemed as vast as the rest of the country put together, and the knowledge that an entire ocean wasn't far away made things seem even bigger. Instead, Clint kept his senses open and his mind on track. Eclipse was smart enough to stick to a trail and skirt the occasional obstacle on his own.

"I think I see someone!" Johnny shouted.

Clint rolled his eyes. The first few times Johnny had made such claims, Clint had taken them seriously. After half a dozen false alarms caused by groundhogs or rabbits, the man driving the wagon had lost just a bit of his credibility.

"Where at, Johnny?" Clint asked, since it was the quickest way to shut him up.

"Over by them rocks. Just up ahead. You see 'em?"

Clint glanced in that direction and replied, "I see the rocks and not much else. You sure it's not just another rabbit?"

"It's not a rabbit!"

Squinting toward an outcropping of large boulders, Clint studied every stony curve and found nothing. "That's just shadows of clouds passing over them."

Johnny made a fretting sound and then said, "Not those rocks! The other ones!"

"What the hell are you talking about, Johnny?" Clint asked as he turned in his saddle to look at the other man's panicked face.

A split second after Clint turned, something hissed through the air and nipped at Clint's ear. Clint's head snapped toward the rocks, and his hand darted up to touch the spot where it felt as if something had bit him. As he fingered the bloody nick on the side of his ear, Clint heard the echo of a rifle work its way through the air.

"Get down!" Clint shouted.

Johnny started to duck, but wasn't able to drop too far while also maintaining control of the horses. "Just let me get to my rifle," he said.

"Turn the horses first!"

Another shot hissed toward Clint, but missed since Eclipse was now weaving in an erratic pattern. The sound of that shot was lost amid the thunder of Eclipse's hooves and the two men's shouting.

Bracing himself with both feet planted firmly against the boards, Johnny pulled hard on the reins to steer the horses to the right. The wagon shuddered and groaned around him, but managed to make the sharp turn without overturning. He did, however, lose a few of his things from the back.

Snatching the rifle from its holster on the side of his saddle, Clint aimed in the direction of the rocks and fired a shot. "Don't ride in a straight line," he shouted to Johnny. "Keep turning, but don't fall into a pattern. That should make it hard enough for them to get a clean shot."

"What about you? I can help you!"

"Just don't get shot," Clint said. "That'll be good enough for me." With that, he hunkered down over Eclipse's back and touched his heels to the stallion's sides. That was all the Darley Arabian needed to launch into a full gallop that sent a rolling thunder through the air.

Ignoring the rocks he'd studied before, Clint turned his sights to another set of rocks that was half the size. The first thing that caught his eye was a horse and rider standing idly by the rocks. As he drew closer, Clint picked out what he thought to be a figure laying on top of the highest rock.

Sighting along the top of his rifle, Clint squeezed off a round and knew he would've had to be blessed to hit anything at all. Even so, he figured he would buy himself at least another few seconds before the other rifle was fired at him.

He figured wrong.

Whoever was laying on top of the rocks wasn't the one who'd fired at him. A puff of smoke appeared in front of the figure on horseback as a round whipped a few feet to Clint's left. The only reason it hadn't hit was because Clint had pulled Eclipse to the right as soon as he'd taken that last shot.

Rather than take his hand from the reins, Clint held the rifle out and swung it by the lever to put the next round into the chamber. He pulled hard on the reins again, steering Eclipse to the left at a less severe angle than his previous turn. The man on horseback ahead of him fired again, but didn't come close enough for Clint to hear the bullet pass by.

Just to be certain, Clint shifted his aim toward the top of the rocks and fired. He may have been jostling too hard to expect a lot of accuracy, but he was now close enough to the rocks to hit them in the correct general area.

The ricochet could be heard, followed by a high-pitched shriek. After that, the figure slid off the back of the rocks and out of Clint's sight.

Since that had worked so well, Clint aimed for another section of rocks and squeezed his trigger. There was another ricochet, followed by the ratchet of Clint levering in another round. He fired again, hitting the same section and causing another piercing ricochet.

The horse that had been standing near the rocks reacted to the second near-miss more than the first and shifted just enough to throw off his rider's aim.

Ignoring the shot, which sailed way over his head, Clint dropped the rifle back into its harness on his saddle and drew his modified Colt. He fired one shot to keep the horse in front of him spooked, but held off on pulling his trigger again when he saw the other rider snap his reins and charge into the fray.

TEN

With the sun beating down so hard on him, Clint thought he was mistaken when he saw something glitter in the rider's hand. More than just light meeting metal, the sparkle seemed more like a reflection thrown by a mirror. He didn't take too much time to think it over, though. After all, he had plenty more to keep him busy at the moment.

The other horse bolted from the spot where it had been standing and took off at a ninety-degree angle from those rocks. Soon, Clint heard another set of hooves beating against the ground. When he took a quick look in that direction, he saw a smaller figure riding away in the opposite direction.

The first rider was obviously a man and he sat tall in the saddle. Once he turned and fired another shot at Clint, he made himself Clint's main target. Clint squeezed off a round, but missed when the man threw himself into an evasive turn similar to the ones Clint, himself, had been using.

Once he was pointed toward the wagon, however, the rider snapped his reins and kept racing in that direction. He fired a few halfhearted shots over his shoulder, but those were mainly to buy some distance between himself and Clint. His rounds came close, which was impressive since he was barely even looking at Clint before shooting at him.

Clint straightened his arm and took a moment to sight along his barrel. He had a clear shot. Unfortunately, it was a clear shot at the rider's back, and that just didn't set well with him. Cursing under his breath, Clint snapped the reins and brought Eclipse around to come in at another angle.

The rider fired once more at the wagon as he dug his heels into his horse's sides. Johnny had taken another sharp turn, but was still refusing to leave Clint too far behind. Extending his arm, the rider took careful aim and raced to put himself in pistol range.

Eclipse tore over the landscape like one of the many bullets that had been fired. He swooped around to the other rider's left and cut across so Clint could try and catch the man's attention.

Not only did Clint catch the rider's attention, but he almost caught a bullet as the man twisted in his saddle and fired in a flicker of motion.

It all happened in the blink of an eye, but froze in Clint's mind.

Clint could see the grin spreading across the man's dark, smooth features. He could see the thin mustache on Franco's upper lip and he could see the fancy gun in the Spaniard's hand. When that gun went off, it seemed more like photographer's flash powder.

When Clint moved, it felt as if his muscles were taking days to respond to his brain's commands. At the core of his being, Clint knew for certain that he wouldn't be able to duck away from that shot. Then, it seemed like the moment was dragging on so long because his mind knew that bright California sky would be the last thing he'd ever see.

Suddenly, Clint's vision was pulled away from the rider and he was nearly thrown from his saddle.

The echo of the gunshot rang in his ears, even though he didn't recall hearing the actual explosion.

Clint tried tightening his grip on the reins, but quickly realized his fingers were already clenched as tightly around the leather straps as they could manage. It took a moment, but he also realized that he hadn't even been hit by the shot that had just been fired.

When he blinked and tried to focus, Clint discovered why he could no longer see the other rider. Eclipse was facing away from the man and had yet to steady his pace. The straining muscles in Clint's arm told him that he was probably the one who'd pulled Eclipse in that direction just before the shot came. However it had happened, the stallion's response had saved Clint's life.

The Darley Arabian shook his head and bobbed it up and down, which soon began to make his steps more and more wobbly. As Eclipse kept shaking his head, blood sprayed through the air over him.

With the bullets still flying in the vicinity of the wagon, Clint did his best to steady Eclipse before the other man found the shot he'd been after.

Franco turned his back to Clint once more and headed toward the wagon. He could only see the back of the vehicle, which gave him nothing worth shooting. Even so, he was well within pistol range, so he kept his gun in hand and steered his horse to get a better angle.

He was hoping to get a look at the wagon's driver, and he got exactly what he'd wanted in a big way. Johnny raised up to look over the top of the wagon. In his hand was a Winchester rifle, which quickly swung around to aim at its target.

Johnny fired the moment Franco was in his sights. Without pausing to see what he'd hit, he chambered another round and fired again.

Hot lead blazed toward Franco from over the top of the slowly moving wagon. When he steered his horse out of the rifle's line of sight, he quickly found himself back in Clint's. The modified Colt barked and sent a round through Franco's flesh. It wasn't a mortal wound, but it hurt enough to make the Spaniard think twice about what he intended on doing.

Reacting out of pure self-preservation, Franco took quick aim at Clint and pulled his trigger. The nickel-plated gun bucked in his hand, and as soon as its round was delivered, Franco turned to aim at the wagon. Johnny had just poked his head up when he saw the pistol swing toward him. He just managed to drop back down again as the .44 barked at him.

Franco saw his opportunity when both men were reacting to those shots. Rather than wait around for Clint and Johnny to recover, Franco steered his horse away from both of them and got the animal moving at a full gallop.

Clint wasn't able to spot Franco right away. His arm moved to keep the modified Colt aiming at whatever he could see. As his eyes snapped back and forth for a hint of where the Spaniard had gone, his hand flinched in that direction as well.

Just as he'd spotted the dust kicked up by Franco's horse, Clint also realized the animals pulling the wagon were turning in his direction. That was more than likely due to the fact that Johnny was firing his rifle wildly from the other side of his seat.

Another shot came in response to the rifle, which Clint immediately recognized as coming from that fancy .44 carried by the man who'd attacked them. The next thing Clint heard was Johnny's voice hollering in pain.

"God damn!" Johnny shouted as he dropped back down into his seat. "I'm hit!"

Clint's first impulse was to ride around the front of the wagon so he could try to catch up to the other rider. The team hitched to the wagon was already spooked enough, so Clint brought Eclipse around to move toward the back of it instead.

As the wagon rolled on and Clint rode across its wake, he could hear the receding thunder of Franco's horse. It wasn't until Clint had ridden all the way around the wagon that he finally managed to catch sight of the horse itself.

This time, Clint wasn't so squeamish about taking a shot at the man's back. He had plenty of time to adjust his aim until he was certain he could drop Franco from his saddle. Before he could pull his trigger, however, another bullet hissed toward Clint from long range.

Clint's blood was racing so hard that he was hugging Eclipse's neck before another round could catch him in the face. But another round didn't come.

Another round wasn't even necessary.

Franco had managed to put a few trees between himself and Clint, which sullied Clint's aim just long enough for Franco to get to the rocks. After that, the Spaniard was gone.

ELEVEN

Clint was examining where Eclipse had been shot. The bullet had clipped the Darley Arabian's ear in much the same way that one of Franco's earlier bullets had clipped Clint's ear. Johnny kept making jokes about Clint sharing his wounds with his horse.

The wagon was stopped near a river and not too far from the main trail. Now that he'd cleaned the blood from Eclipse's ear, Clint knelt down to see about cleaning himself up. Blood had formed a thick crust on his ear, making it looked like it had been chewed off rather than shot. Washing away some of that crust, Clint got down to the wound itself. He winced when he dripped some water on it, but at least his ear felt closer to the way he remembered it.

Resting with his back against a rock beside the river, Johnny shifted and winced in pain. His shirt had been stripped away, and his chest was wrapped up with several layers of bandages. Actually, the bandages were the shredded remains of one of the bags Johnny had packed and tossed into the back of the wagon. They hadn't been around him long, but the makeshift bandages were already soaked through with blood.

Clint dabbed at his ear and took a look at Johnny.

"Looks like the bleeding might have stopped. At any rate, we should probably let that wound breathe for a bit."

Letting out a wary sigh, Johnny grabbed a knife that was sticking out of the ground and started to cut the bandages.

"Here," Clint said as he stepped forward. "Better let me do that."

"You had to do the stitches and listen to me cuss at you the whole time, so I figure I should start being a bigger help."

"I've heard plenty worse."

Clint took the knife and carefully sliced the bandages so he could peel them away. The wound was better than it had been when they'd first found the river, but it was still seeping blood. After washing some of the blood away, Clint examined the stitches and handed the canteen over to Johnny.

"How's it look?" Johnny asked, refusing to look down at himself.

"Let's just say that Eclipse and I got the better end of the bargain."

When Johnny laughed, he quickly winced and forced himself to stay still.

"Are those stitches going to hold?" Clint asked.

"I think so. Where'd you learn your doctoring?"

"I'd like to tell you it's something I was taught by a very wise man. The truth is that I get a lot of practice from all the people trying to carve out a piece of me for themselves."

"Well, you did a fine job. It still hurts like a bastard, though."

"I'll bet it does. By the looks of it, the bullet dug in about half an inch all the way across. You're damn lucky to be alive."

Johnny took as deep a breath as he could and let it out. "I sure don't feel lucky."

"You have any whiskey?"

Suddenly, Johnny's eyes lit up. "In my wagon, just behind the seat."

"That explains your skill with the reins."

"Go to hell, Clint. But first, go get my whiskey."

Clint was still chuckling when he returned with the bottle. Considering how bad Johnny looked when they'd brought the horses to a stop, Clint was awfully glad that the man was still alive. For that matter, taking a grazing shot to the ear for himself seemed like a fairly light sentence.

"Thanks, Clint. And not just for this," Johnny said as he held up the bottle. "If it wasn't for you, I wouldn't be breathing right now. I sure as hell wouldn't still have my gold."

"That's funny. I was just thinking what a piss-poor job I did in keeping you safe."

Johnny shook his head while tilting the bottle to his lips. As the whiskey flowed through his system, his voice was less strained and his posture became a bit more relaxed.

"If you hadn't did what you done, that first rifle shot would have taken me down."

"I'm lucky that first rifle shot didn't put me down."

After pondering that for a moment, Johnny shrugged. "Maybe, but everything after that was pure guts. I've never seen the like."

"You pulled your share when that rider came in close. I didn't even see what happened."

"I saw someone ride up to me and it took me a second to realize it wasn't you. Soon as I saw that gun in his hand coming at me, I fired a shot that didn't even come close to hitting a damn thing. I . . . lost my balance and started to fall. That must've been when he pulled his trigger, because I felt like my chest was tore off. With all the blood that came out of me, he must have thought he killed me." Shaking his head, he added, "Then he rode away."

"That's nothing to be ashamed of," Clint said after picking up on the tremor in Johnny's voice.

"Well . . . actually I didn't fall. I dropped to save my own hide. All that while you were still fighting." Johnny shook his head and took another pull from the whiskey bottle.

"You would have been stupid if you weren't scared back there," Clint told him. "It's just like I said. Nothing to be ashamed of."

"What about you? Were you scared?"

Without missing a beat, Clint replied, "Hell no! You think I'm yellow?"

There was just enough bluster in Clint's voice to make Johnny laugh rather than cringe. In fact, Johnny laughed so hard that he wound up pressing a hand against his chest and forcing himself to calm down before he busted a stitch.

Once Johnny caught his breath, Clint asked, "Do you think you'll be able to move soon? We should find someplace to stash this wagon before anyone comes around looking for us."

"I won't be flapping my arms or nothing, but I should be able to hold the reins."

"Good."

"You think he's coming back?"

"I'd guess so," Clint replied. "Especially since both of us rode away from there with the gold. Otherwise, there wasn't much sense in them ambushing us in the first place."

"So they were after the gold?"

"Unless you're carrying any diamonds or rare pieces of art in that wagon, I'd say the gold is the most valuable thing you've got."

Johnny rolled his eyes and nodded. "Good point. Maybe I've had a bit too much of this whiskey."

"Did that man look familiar to you?" Clint asked.

At first, Johnny shook his head. Then, he cocked his head a bit and said, "You know, I might have seen that fella at my party."

"Was he with anyone?"

"Just some pretty Mexican lady with long hair. You think she's a part of this?"

"I don't know. I just hope he was some asshole who overheard something at the party and decided to make a play for it."

"Why?" Johnny grunted. "Isn't that bad enough?"

Clint's hand reflexively lowered to rest upon his holstered Colt. "No. It can get a whole lot worse than that."

TWELVE

Franco sat hunched over as Rosa rubbed her hands along his back. Dusk was setting in, and the shadows were growing just enough for the firelight to bring out the angles in his face. As the flames crackled and sent the occasional ember sailing off, Franco prodded the wood at the heart of the fire with a thick branding iron.

"At least you killed one of them," Rosa said in a consoling tone.

Franco's lips curled into a sneer as if forming the words before he spoke them. "I might have killed him. All I know is that I hit the one on the wagon."

"What about Adams? You must have hit him, too."

"Perhaps."

"Oh, come now," she cooed as her hands worked on loosening the knots in his muscles. "I've never seen you miss a shot like that. He didn't even know you were there. You must have hit him."

"Perhaps," he repeated impatiently.

"If you didn't kill them, then are you . . . just going to let them go?"

Franco wheeled around as if he meant to take a swing at her. Just as he caught sight of Rosa, his face twisted into a pained grimace and he turned back around. "I'm not going to let them go," he said. "I'll just have to catch up to them at a different spot."

Eventually, Rosa's hands found their way back to Franco's shoulders. She caressed him at first, but then began to massage him once more. "I didn't mean to doubt you."

"I know."

"You should probably see to that wound before it gets any worse."

Slowly, Franco nodded. Even now, he couldn't remember exactly when he'd been hit. He was certain, however, that the bullet had come from Clint's gun. Picturing Clint's face as he lifted the branding iron from the bottom of the fire, Franco pulled in a breath and pressed the hottest end of the iron against his side.

His flesh hissed and steamed the moment it made contact with the iron. Every muscle in Franco's body squirmed beneath his skin, and even Rosa's hands weren't enough to soothe him. He kept the iron there for as long as he could bear it. After a few seconds, the searing heat started to feel cold.

"That's it," Rosa said. "Now take it away."

Franco started to take the iron away, but quickly discovered the tip was stuck to his skin. Before the iron became seared into him any deeper, Franco pulled and twisted it away at the same time. That pulled a bit of meat off, but still left the main wound mostly shut. Before he lowered the iron, Rosa was reaching around to place a moist rag against him.

"That's better, isn't it?" she asked soothingly.

Franco nodded slowly. He didn't need to look at the wound to know how bad it was. The bullet had passed through when it had been fired. He knew that much already. Since the wound was too jagged to be stitched up easily, he'd opted for the more painful method of using the iron.

As Rosa pressed down and then removed the rag, she replaced it with another one. "Can you feel that?" she asked.

"No."

"Good." Before he had too much time to think about what he did feel, she asked, "What are you going to do next?"

"In the morning, we will ride ahead to that bank. We shouldn't have any trouble getting there before they do."

"Won't there be a lot of people there?"

"It is a small town. We should have no trouble spotting them and picking them off before they reach a main street."

Rosa nodded and removed the rag to look at the charred flesh beneath it. The bleeding had stopped, and though the wound wasn't very pretty, at least it was no longer open. "That could get dangerous."

Snapping his head around to glare at her with fire in his eyes, Franco knocked Rosa back and started to crawl toward her. "You don't think I know that?"

Scooting away from him and the fire, Rosa kept quiet.

Although his draw was a bit slower than normal, Franco's .44 still cleared leather in the blink of an eye. He pointed the gun straight at her at first, but then held it so she could see it from the side as he snarled, "You think I could have earned this without knowing how, where, and when to kill a man?"

Rosa's eyes were drawn along the etched nickel plating and lingered on the gem embedded in the handle. The sapphire was set into the grip amid a swirl of elegant carvings. The more she looked at it, the more it seemed the sapphire was floating in a pool of silver.

"Do you?" Franco demanded.

That brought her eyes back to his and she replied, "No."

Suddenly, Franco recoiled and lowered the pistol. He looked at her face and then quickly turned away. After that, he backed up almost enough for his boots to dip into the bottom of the campfire. "I apologize," he said.

Moving up behind him as if nothing had happened, Rosa draped her arms over his shoulders so she could brush her hands along the Spaniard's chest. "You're hurt and you're upset," she whispered into his ear. "I understand."

"I will not let them get away again. I underestimated Adams." Gritting his teeth, Franco picked up a nearby twig and snapped it angrily. "Knowing what I know about him, I still underestimated him," he said while pitching pieces of the twig into the flames. "That was just stupid."

Rosa's hands slid under his shirt, which hung open loosely to reveal several old scars that looked just as twisted and melted as the new one. "You're not stupid," she purred.

Franco closed his eyes and focused on the way Rosa's fingers glided over his skin. He thought about the way her breasts pressed against his back and the way her legs slowly rubbed against him as she settled in behind him.

The more she touched him, the more focused his thoughts became. By the time he turned and crawled on top of her, Franco could already feel his target's blood on his hands.

THIRTEEN

Dover Shallows wasn't a big town by any stretch of the imagination, but it was pretty enough to look as though it had been painted rather than built. Four of the main streets formed a square, while a fifth street cut through the middle. Everything else was built around that simple design. There were some shops, a few restaurants, and only one saloon. And, located directly across from the marshal's office, there was a bank.

Shallows State Bank actually resembled one of the restaurants, right down to the decorative curls built into the awnings and shutters. It was painted white and green to match the well-kept rows of flowers planted along the front walk.

Folks in Dover Shallows all seemed happy to be there. Even though his wound was still aching and gave him hell every time he moved the wrong way, Franco was also happy to be there. He stood outside a restaurant called Minnie's, which was across the street and down a little ways from the bank. From there, he could pat his belly as if he was still full from lunch and tip his hat to all the other happy folks who walked by. More than a few women let their eyes linger on Franco's handsome face, and he rewarded them with a gleaming smile.

Franco checked his pocket watch and then snapped it shut. According to his calculations, Johnny Blevin should have arrived to make his deposit a little while ago. There was always the possibility that he'd been hurt even worse than Franco thought, but that was probably overly optimistic.

Thinking back to the last shot he'd fired at Johnny, Franco recalled every second, the way a young man might dwell on memories of the first time he'd bedded a woman. Franco could remember every sound and every movement. The sight of Johnny reeling back onto the wagon's driver seat was embedded in those memories.

There had been a lot of blood spilled by that shot. In fact, there had been a little too much blood spilled. Given how far Johnny was twisted to one side, Franco became even more convinced that his bullet had been a messy grazing shot, at best. Since he hadn't found a trace of the wagon or Adams the morning after he'd had a chance to tend his own wound, Franco knew both men had most likely made it.

All of this had flown through Franco's mind by the time his watch had hit the bottom of his pocket. When he looked up again, he caught sight of another passerby in the corner of his eye.

Only, this one didn't pass by.

Instead, the figure stayed at the edge of Franco's field of vision. Before Franco could turn to tip his hat, he felt the distinctive touch of a gun barrel tap against his back.

"If you think I'm still against shooting you in the back," Clint said softly, "you're more than welcome to put me to the test."

Franco remained still. His casual smile even remained plastered onto his face. "Not a very private place for an execution," he pointed out.

"No, but it is a fine spot to nab a bank robber."

"I had no plans on robbing a bank."

"And if I marched you into that marshal's office, he wouldn't recognize your face or that fancy gun of yours in connection to any other wrongdoings of late?" Clint asked.

Turning just enough to look over his shoulder at Clint, Franco put an extra dose of smugness into his smile and replied, "I'd be more than happy to visit the marshal. My guess is that you have more kills associated with your name than I do."

Clint paused to allow another pair of locals to walk past Minnie's.

"And I am not the one holding a man at gunpoint right now," Franco said confidently. "If I raise my voice, I might even be able to get you arrested."

"You won't do that," Clint said. "Because then you wouldn't be able to pick Johnny off before he could deposit his money. Actually, I'm surprised to find you here rather than watching the roads from farther out. But that's what your partner was supposed to be doing, right?"

Hearing that last part, Franco turned slightly around and was stopped by Clint's gun.

Clint knew he'd struck a nerve, so he struck one more time with "She's got a good eye. I'll bet she's a great scout. She is only human, though, which means she can't look in every direction at once. But you know how that feels right about now, don't you?"

"If you think I'm going to let slip where she is, you're sadly mistaken."

"I'm not trying to get you to say anything," Clint stated. "I figured you knew where we were headed, otherwise you would have hit Johnny earlier on. It would have been messier, but you can afford to pick your shot when you know where your target is going.

"Rather than race you to this town, I thought it would be

more sociable if I just met you here. Unfortunately, Johnny isn't around for this little reunion."

Franco let out a sigh and grunted, "You're enjoying this, aren't you, Adams?"

"After your little ambush, yeah. I am enjoying watching you squirm a bit."

"So, I have squirmed," Franco said as though he were squatting down in the muck to speak at Clint's level. "What will you do now?"

"I'm going to escort you out of town and away from these good people and make sure you aren't able to lift a finger to hamper Johnny from making his deposit."

"Fine. Let's go."

Clint nudged Franco with his gun barrel to make sure the Spaniard was moving in the right direction. Once Franco was walking on his own, Clint quickly holstered the Colt without making a sound and nodded to an elderly woman crossing the street to go into the bank.

As far as anyone else was concerned, Clint and Franco were just two amiable fellows out for a stroll.

FOURTEEN

Clint and Franco didn't speak as they walked down the second of Dover Shallows's main streets. Every so often, Franco would test the waters by slowing his pace or looking for a spot where he could split away from Clint. Every errant glance or pause in his stride was met by a subtle prod from the barrel of Clint's modified Colt.

Since he was able to keep Franco in front of him, Clint could keep his gun holstered throughout most of his walk. Whenever he needed to put Franco back on track, he drew the gun, used it to give the Spaniard a shove, and holstered it again before anyone else noticed.

Once they got away from the main streets, however, they both had a bit more room to breathe.

Franco planted his feet and came to a stop in an empty lot behind a livery filled with wagons and carts in various stages of repair. He kept his hands at his sides and his eyes pointed straight ahead.

"I'm not walking another step," Franco announced.

"That's up to you."

Although he knew Clint couldn't see it, Franco smiled. "Then I suppose you wouldn't mind if I walked to my horse, rode away, and our paths never crossed again?"

"Actually, that sounds nice." After allowing Franco to take one step, Clint added, "But you and I both know that's not how it will happen."

Slowly, Franco turned around to face Clint. Every fraction of every second that it took for him to do so grated on Franco's nerves like a rake across a chalkboard. Despite being a little surprised to complete the turn, Franco put on a victorious grin. "You never took my gun from me."

Clint calmly nodded. "I know."

"This was never about you, Adams."

"I know that, too. I got a vested interest in this from the moment you started shooting at me. That's not something any man would let pass so easily."

"Especially not a man like you."

"No," Clint said gravely. "Especially not a man like me."

Franco stood his ground and let his hand move to his holster. Although he didn't make an attempt to draw his .44, he brushed his fingers past it just to make certain it hadn't been taken from him somewhere along the way.

The .44 was still there.

As Franco's hand lingered near the holstered pistol, he saw Clint's hand tensing as it eased its way to his own Colt. Franco raising his arm until his hand was held straight out in front of him was enough to get Clint to relax just a bit.

"This can go on for a long time," Franco mused.

"It doesn't have to. Not so long as you drop that holster and come with me without making a fuss."

The Spaniard smiled once more and nodded. "Ah yes. I have heard this about you. You will give a man the chance to walk away before you gun him down. At least, that is how the story goes."

"Not every man gets that choice," Clint pointed out. "Only the ones who don't force my hand."

"And you would forgive our little scuffle from before?"

"No, but I wouldn't have to kill you."

"And where would we go?" Franco asked.

"I know some U.S. marshals not far from here. Since you strike me as someone who might have a badge or two watching your back, I'd prefer to take you to someone I can trust."

"If I had bought the law in this town, I would not have needed to be so careful, no?"

Clint shrugged. "Maybe. I'd still rather do it my way to be sure."

"And how do I know you would hand me over to a lawman I could trust? Or that I would even make it there alive?"

"Because, if I'd wanted you dead, you'd already be facedown in the dirt."

Franco's eyes narrowed and he pulled in a slow breath. When he let that breath out, it was in a short, decisive sigh. "I think not, Adams." With that, the Spaniard snapped his hand toward his holster and pulled the .44 from its spot.

Clint's arm moved in a similar flicker of motion as his hand was suddenly wrapped around his modified Colt.

Both weapons cleared leather at the same time, but Clint was able to aim and pull his trigger before Franco's hammer could drop. The Colt barked once and sent a bullet through Franco's heart. The .44 roared as well, but only after a twitching reflex of Franco's finger.

The Spaniard had a surprised look on his face as the fire in his eyes slowly dwindled away. He started to wobble backward, but was spun around as Clint's second shot punched through his shoulder.

As promised, Franco's body landed facedown in the dirt.

FIFTEEN

Rosa laid on her back in the same spot where Clint and Johnny had found her. The hill was a little ways outside of town and had a good view of nearly every side of Dover Shallows. It also had a real good view of all three roads that led into town.

She could feel the rumble of approaching hooves and winced when that rumble got so close that she got fresh dust kicked in her face when Eclipse skidded to a halt. Straining her neck to get a look at the new arrival, Rosa was only given a closer look at the business end of Johnny's rifle.

"I told you not to move, bitch," Johnny snarled as he leaned down and pressed the rifle barrel against her forehead.

Tears formed in her eyes as she looked up at him and did her best to nod.

Johnny looked up for a moment and asked, "Did you find the other one?"

"Yeah," Clint said as he climbed down from the saddle. Walking to stand next to Rosa, Clint made sure she could see his face when he added, "He's dead."

"Really?" Rosa asked anxiously. She was so anxious, in

59

fact, that she caused Johnny to lean in and shove her head down once more.

Clint looked at the top of the hill, which was mostly flat and only big enough to possibly support one more horse before forcing someone to stand at an incline. Laying well out of reach were the things that had been on Rosa's person when Clint had snuck up on her upon his arrival.

Most prominent among her possessions was a large shotgun. The shells for the shotgun were scattered on the ground, and a spyglass laid nearby as well. The only other things Rosa had when she'd been searched were the clothes on her back.

"Has she been behaving?" Clint asked.

Reluctantly, Johnny nodded. "She asked to sit up a few times, but I didn't let her. Other than that, it's been pretty quiet."

Rosa started to speak, but was cut short by a warning glare from Clint. She closed her mouth and even tried to press her head back further against the grass when she saw Clint kneel down and lean in closer to her.

Keeping one hand on his Colt, Clint used the other hand to pat her down. Since her blouse was off both shoulders, there wasn't much of a need to search too high. He placed his hand flat against her torso and felt quickly around and between her breasts. He moved his hand down to feel her waist and then patted along both legs. His touch was quick and precise without lingering in any one spot for too long. Only after he felt for a holster or scabbard in her boots did Clint relax.

Just to be certain, Clint sifted his fingers through her hair. He found a single decorative comb toward the back of her head, which he removed and tossed away.

"All right," Clint said to Johnny. "Let her up."

"Are you sure?"

"If she's got something I didn't find, she won't be able to get to it before one of us puts her down."

Nodding, Johnny eased back and took a few shuffling steps away from her. He still kept his rifle to his shoulder and his sights on Rosa.

"That doesn't look too comfortable," Clint said. "Why don't you sit up?"

After glancing to Johnny to make sure he wasn't going to shoot, Rosa sat up and shifted until she was fairly comfortable. "Thank you," she said to Clint.

"Don't thank me. You're not out of this yet."

Her eyes widened a bit and she recoiled. "I was just along with him, I swear. I didn't even have a choice."

"You were here acting as his lookout," Clint pointed out. "That makes you an accomplice in anyone's book."

"I stayed out here," she insisted. "I may have shared a bed with him, but I would never take part in a killing."

Clint picked up one of the shotgun shells and rolled it in his palm. Since Johnny hadn't let his guard down yet, Clint took a moment to pull out the innards of the shell and dump them into his hand. "There's twice the amount of powder in this and no buckshot," he said. "Not too deadly, but it would make one hell of a noise. Probably loud enough to be heard in town if someone knew what to listen for."

"Son of a bitch," Johnny said under his breath. Narrowing his eyes to glare down at Rosa, he snarled, "You were gonna tip that killer off as to when we got here."

She was shaking her head before all of Johnny's accusation had even escaped his lips. "No, I swear! Well . . . that's what I was supposed to do, but I didn't have a choice. He would've killed me if I didn't!" The tears were flowing freely down her cheeks now, and her voice was burdened by a growing number of sobs. "He would've killed me."

Clint hunkered down to her level and looked her in the eyes. He ignored Rosa's tears, the sobs that wracked her shoulders, and even her desperate pleas. Instead, he focused on her eyes. They were bloodshot and swelling with tears, but still gave him something to work with when he asked, "Why should we believe a damn word you say?"

"Because it's the truth."

"You're telling me you couldn't have just run away rather than lay up here on this hill all by yourself?"

"Where should I go? I've tried running before and he only found me. When he did . . . it was . . . bad." She sniffled and wiped her eyes with the heel of her hand. "It was real bad. He promised I wouldn't survive it if I ran again, and I believe him."

"That don't make sense," Johnny grunted. "Why the hell would an assassin drag around some crying woman?"

"Answer the question," Clint said. "I'd like to hear the answer myself."

"I . . . did things for him," she replied. "Helped him. He paid me and I was safe so long as I did what I was told. There's a whole lot worse jobs out there."

"What about now that your partner is dead?" Clint asked. "Are you willing to help us?"

"He's not my partner," she said vehemently. Slowly, a bit of hope shone in her eyes. "Is he really dead?"

Clint straightened up, reached for a bundle wedged beneath his shirt and waistband, and then tossed the bundle to the ground. The nickel-plated .44 landed with a solid thump.

Rosa started to reach for it, but quickly pulled her hand back.

"Go on and take a look," Clint said. "It's not loaded."

She reached for it again. This time, however, her hand stopped less than an inch shy of grabbing the handle. Gritting her teeth, she took hold of the gun and seemed almost too weak to pick it up. Once she hefted its weight, she turned it over and looked at the sapphire embedded into the grip.

"It's really his gun," she said. "He must be dead."

"Isn't that what I told you?" Clint asked.

Handing the pistol back, she looked up at Clint with wide, tear-streaked eyes. "What do you want me to do?"

"I want you to answer some questions. But not here. We've got some riding to do before it gets dark."

SIXTEEN

Rosa had her hands tied to the saddle horn of her horse. Actually, it wasn't her horse, but one of the animals that had been pulling Johnny's wagon. She did a good job of keeping her balance, but it took a good deal of concentration as the terrain started to get more and more uneven. "Where are you taking me?" she asked while shifting to keep from falling.

Johnny rode beside her with his reins in one hand and his rifle in the other. Rosa's reins were tied around his saddle horn. "We're going to get my wagon, if you must know," he replied. "After that, I'm finishing up my business."

"You mean we're going back to that bank? Are you sure that's a good idea?"

"You don't have a say in it," Johnny snapped. "I'll do what I need to do and I don't need your say-so to do it!"

From behind both of them, Clint shouted, "We're not going to that bank."

Johnny's head snapped back so quickly that it almost looked like it was going to come off his shoulders. "What?"

"There are plenty of other banks in the country, Johnny. You know that, right?"

"Yeah, but my money's in . . ." Johnny paused and shot a glance over to Rosa. "You know."

"So does she, remember? No need to speak in codes."

After grumbling incoherently under his breath, Johnny said, "Well, I don't like this idea. That bank is a damn good one and I want a place I can trust."

"And what if something happened to that bank?" Clint asked. "Like, for example, an assassin tried to kill you walking into it one day?"

"Smart ass."

"It's a good idea to use more than one bank. Believe me, I've been doing it for years. Keeps the bad element like that lady over there and her friends from getting their hands on your valuables."

"Do you know a place I can trust?"

"I've got one in mind right now, as a matter of fact."

"What about her?" Johnny asked as he nodded toward Rosa. "What if she gets word as to where the rest of her assassin friends should go next?"

Rosa hung her head low, but didn't say a word in her own defense.

"She won't tell anybody about it," Clint said confidently.

That brought a similar look of surprise to both of the others' faces. The only difference was that Rosa also had a touch of fear in her eyes.

After letting those previous words sink in, Clint added, "Because she'll be in jail by then. But first, she's going to talk to us about her assassin friends."

Rosa shifted in her saddle so she could look at Clint. It wasn't easy because of the ropes tying her wrists, but she was able to see Clint's face when she asked, "Are you going to set me free if I tell you enough?"

"No."

"Then why should I say anything else?"

"Because," Clint replied, "there are plenty of different types of jails you can go to. I could take you to the U.S.

Marshals, who I know work down to the letter of the law, or I could take you to a few sheriffs I know who don't hinder themselves as much with rules and regulations."

Johnny looked over to Clint as well. He studied Clint's face to see if he could tell how much of what Clint was saying was actually going to be backed up by action. He got as much information from Clint's expression as Rosa did, which was absolutely none.

"Even someone who rides along with killers should know the type of men I'm talking about," Clint said. "They'd be the sort of lawmen who your friend with the fancy gun would have avoided like the plague because they tend to take walks when the vigilantes come by. They're the kind who may even save themselves the trouble of a court trial by just cleaning out their cells since they know the people in them will hang either way."

Having kept his face relatively blank until now, Clint met Rosa's stare directly and put an icy edge into his voice when he said, "They're also the type who'd love to know they had a real assassin in their jail. Killers like that make them look real good, come election time. I don't even think they'd mind if you pulled the trigger or just came along for the ride. Some lawmen hate people like you even more. Your friend was doing a job. You were just along for the ride and watching innocent folks die."

Finally, Rosa couldn't take any more. "Enough," she said as she took her eyes off of Clint and lowered her head. "I don't want to hear any more."

"Then tell me something I want to hear."

"Like what?"

"Start with the name of your partner."

"Franco Dominguez," she replied softly.

"All right. Now, who hired you to kill me and Johnny?"

"They didn't hire me," she said softly.

When Clint spoke again, the edge was no longer in his

voice. In fact, he seemed comforting as he corrected himself. "Sorry. I meant when they hired your . . . employer."

Rosa looked up to find Clint riding directly beside her now. He smiled and nodded to let her know that she was out of harm's way for the moment.

"What was his name?" Clint asked.

Rosa kept her head hung low. The only movement she made was due to the horse moving beneath her.

"What about your name?" Clint asked.

After a few seconds, she uttered, "Rosa."

"Do yourself and me a favor, Rosa. Tell me who hired Franco's services, so this whole mess can be through."

Closing her eyes, Rosa let out a breath as if she was convinced it would be her last. "His name was Galloway. That's all I remember."

"That's plenty," Clint said.

SEVENTEEN

They rode all day and a little into the night. When Clint finally signaled for them to make camp, Johnny and Rosa were both about ready to drop over from exhaustion. It hadn't been a rough ride, but they'd spent every waking moment tensed up and ready for trouble. Rosa was ready to feel the sting of Johnny's rifle, and Johnny was ready for her to make a break for freedom.

As the fire sputtered beneath the remnants of their hastily prepared supper, Johnny stretched out and immediately drifted to sleep. That left Clint sitting with his back to a tree and a dented cup of coffee in his hand. His eyes never strayed far from Rosa, even as she laid on her side and tried to get some sleep.

After less than an hour, she woke up again. Rosa turned to look at Clint and found him still sipping his coffee. "How do you do it?" she asked.

"Do what?"

"Keep your eyes open after everything that happened today."

"Because I have to."

"I'm not going anywhere." Holding up her hands,

which were still tied at the wrists, she tugged on the rope that connected her wrists to another tree. "See?"

"Better safe than sorry."

Rosa got her legs beneath her and walked toward Clint. She didn't even make it to the fire before she literally reached the end of her rope. "Could you come over here?" she asked.

"Why?"

"Because I'd like to talk rather than shout."

Rather than make her insist any more, Clint got up and moved closer to her. He sat down just outside of her reach. "What do you want to say?"

"Just that I'm not as bad as you think I am."

"How do you know what I'm thinking?" Clint asked.

"I can see it in your eyes. You and your friend think I'm just as bad as Franco."

"Say whatever you want about being forced or doing what you needed to do, the both of you did try to kill us."

"I know and I'm sorry. I'm so sorry."

Sipping his coffee and blinking once, Clint asked, "Is that all you wanted to say?"

All of the wind was taken from Rosa's sails, causing her shoulders to slump and her head to hang low as it had when they'd been riding. "I guess. I just . . . I just don't want to hang for sharing a bed with a killer."

"You'll be handed over to honest lawmen and you'll get a fair trial. That's all I can guarantee you."

"Will you testify for me?" she asked hopefully.

Clint chuckled under his breath. "I doubt that would help your case much."

"You could tell them what you saw. You know I wasn't the one firing at you. Franco was the one who ambushed you, and he was the one waiting to kill your friend. That's the truth and you know it."

"If I'm asked to testify, I will."

She smiled and nodded. "Thank you. I know it would help."

"Now why don't you get some sleep?"

Despite the fact that she could barely hold her head up or keep her eyes open, Rosa would not lay down. "Will you stay close until the trial?"

"Look . . . I'll do what I can, but—"

"Please. You need to stay close or they'll kill me."

"Who will?"

"The people Franco worked for," Rosa replied.

Clint sighed and finished his last sip of coffee before tossing the cup to the saddlebag laying nearby. "It's too late for this, Rosa. Whatever you're trying to sell me, it won't be enough for me to let you go."

"I'm not trying to sell you anything and I'm not trying to get you to let me go." Shaking her head, Rosa added, "I'm probably safer here with you than anywhere else. Including jail."

"Who's got you so frightened?"

"I don't even know how many of them there are. All I do know is that they're a group of killers who are some of the best money can buy. They call themselves the Sapphire Club."

"Sounds like a saloon I went to in Nevada."

"Not many people even know them by that name. The only time I heard about it was when Franco was bragging about where he got his gun. He told me he was one of the best they had, and if I ever thought about turning against him, they would come for me even if he couldn't.

"Some nights, I thought about killing him when he slept," Rosa confided. "But . . . then I thought about how far I would have to run just to get away from those others. Franco was bad, but I knew I could eventually get him to let me go. Those others are ruthless."

"How do you know for certain?"

"Because they were the only ones who Franco ever had any faith in. Sometimes, I even think he was scared of them."

"Do you know where I can find these others?" Clint asked.

Rosa nodded. "I know where they would meet Franco to give him his jobs." Lifting her chin a bit, she added, "I can take you there."

"Why don't you tell me where it is?"

Although Rosa started to speak, she bit her lip and quickly shook her head. "Not unless I know you can protect me."

"All right, then. We can wait until you're safe and sound, surrounded by some lawmen who can protect you no matter what gets thrown at you. The place we're headed has just those sorts of men. You'll like them."

Clint got up and walked back to the spot where he'd been sitting before. He didn't let Rosa out of his sight, but he also didn't engage her in any more conversation. He merely stayed put, watched the camp, and kept quiet until it was time for Johnny to wake up and take his place.

The next morning, Clint woke up and immediately checked on the other two. Rosa was laying on her side with her back to him and Johnny was using a small mirror and a straightedge to shave himself.

"You're up early," Johnny said. "I wasn't gonna wake you for another few hours."

Clint walked a few more steps from the camp and motioned for Johnny to follow him. Lowering his voice, Clint said, "Rosa and I had a little talk last night."

Stopping in mid-stroke, Johnny took the blade from his cheek and asked, "What about?"

Clint filled him in on the details while making sure Rosa wasn't watching them. He also kept his voice down so she couldn't hear enough to put too much together. By the time he was finished, Johnny was wiping his razor against his knee to clean it off.

"What should we do about this?" Johnny asked.

"I just thought you'd want to know. There might be some interested parties once word gets out that Franco missed his mark."

"Do you think I should go after them?"

Clint smiled and tried not to look too amused by that prospect. "No. I was thinking that you might want to do some traveling until this blows over. Once it's clear that you and your gold are long gone, any hired guns will cut their losses and take another paying job rather than devote their lives to finding one that got away."

Johnny nodded good-naturedly. "You know something? I've always wanted to see England."

Patting Johnny's shoulder, Clint said, "There are a few taverns in London I can highly recommend."

EIGHTEEN

The next stop they made was to pick up Johnny's wagon. Since they'd needed to make better time if they were going to get to Dover Shallows without drawing attention, Clint had convinced Johnny to leave everything behind. Clint knew it was going to be a tough job and he'd been right. Of course, now that they were going back to the wagon, Johnny set the pace fast enough that they made it in record time.

"I just hope it's still there," Johnny fretted as they approached the riverbed just upstream from where he and Clint had tended to their wounds not long ago. Turning to Rosa, Johnny asked, "Did you and that assassin friend of yours find my wagon?"

"No."

"I don't believe you."

"Then shut up until we get there," Clint snapped. "Grousing about it won't do any good."

Johnny held his breath and didn't fully let it out until he spotted a large shape covered mostly by branches stuck into a few large quilts. The cover wasn't perfect, but it kept the wagon out of sight well enough. Johnny snapped his reins and bolted toward the wagon.

Clint, on the other hand, tied the reins of Rosa's horse to a tree and rode toward the sound of running water. He swung down from the saddle, waded knee-deep in the cool water, and stuck his hands into the river.

"Everything looks good," Johnny shouted. "'Cept for a raccoon that I just . . . can't . . . reach. What about you?" When he didn't hear anything right away, Johnny started running toward Clint. "You find 'em?"

Finally, Clint's fingers brushed against the flat rocks he'd stacked there previously. When he pulled them up, they made a wet sucking sound as the underwater mud hole began filling itself in. "I think the water might have washed them away," he replied.

Johnny's voice became shrill with panic. "What? How!? Are you sure?!"

Laughing while straining to lift one of the rectangular boxes out of the water, Clint said, "I'm joking. These damn things are too heavy for a flood to wash them away."

"And they're all still there?"

"Yes. Now, come and help me!"

Johnny opened the boxes and counted up his gold one more time. After that, he hitched the horse he'd been riding back to the wagon and got it ready to roll. Part of that duty was picking through the belongings he'd packed on the wagon and deciding what he should leave behind. His single horse might have been able to get the wagon going, but Johnny was a little more concerned about speed after all that had happened of late.

"I think that quilt is done for," Clint said. "We had to cut it up pretty good to get those branches to stay. You might just want to get rid of it."

"Are you kidding? That quilt did one hell of a job in keeping this wagon out of sight. That means it's lucky as hell!"

"It also means those two probably didn't ride anywhere

close to here," Clint said. "Otherwise, they would have seen this eyesore from a mile away."

"Yeah, but they still wouldn't have gotten my gold." Johnny looked over to Rosa and smirked victoriously. "I'm glad you could see this," he said to her. "I'm still alive, I got my gold, and I'm free as a bird."

Already back in his saddle, Clint rode over to Johnny and held out his hand. "All right then, birdie. Fly away to where we discussed and I'll wrap things up with this lady."

Johnny shook Clint's hand. "You sure you don't want me along till you drop her off? You know, just to watch your back?"

"I'd feel better without having to worry about keeping you safe in case any more of her friends came along. Besides, we're only going to Carson City."

Looking over to where Rosa waited, Johnny said, "Watch yourself with her. Whether she held a gun or not, it don't mean she should be trusted."

"I don't trust her. That's why she's going to jail."

"And where's that jail?"

"Carson City."

Johnny furrowed his brow and grumbled, "That's a ways from here."

"I know someone I can trust who can take her off my hands," Clint said as he nodded toward Rosa.

"You sure you can trust him?"

"Tom's had a few chances to let me down, but he wound up saving my skin instead. It's been a while since I've seen him, but he should remember me well enough. He's also not the sort to mistreat a prisoner."

"Don't tell me you're going soft on her."

Clint chuckled and shook his head. "Not hardly. I also don't have enough reason to hand her over to a pack of wolves."

"Or vigilantes?" Johnny asked.

"Same difference."

"Just keep an eye on her, Clint. It'll take a while to get to Carson City from here."

"Not the way we'll be riding. I appreciate your concern, but I'll be fine. Just take care of yourself and enjoy your trip."

"I will," Johnny said as he reached behind him and took a small bundle from under his seat. "And here's a little something for ya."

The moment Clint took the bundle in his hand, he knew what it was. Wrapped loosely in a wet rag, the bundle was slightly larger than a pack of cards and ten times as heavy. He flipped open the rag and saw the glitter of gold underneath it.

"Thanks, Johnny," Clint said.

"Put that away before anything happens to it."

Clint did just that, and when he turned back around, he saw Johnny holding out another bundle of the same size and shape.

"Go on and take it," Johnny insisted. "I only wish it could be more."

Knowing it would have been a waste of time to refuse the bonus, Clint took the gold and tipped his hat. "Good luck, friend."

"You, too," Johnny said as he got his wagon moving. "With that lady at your side, you're gonna need it."

NINETEEN

For a man like Johnny, who was used to doing most of his travel by wagon, it would have been a long ride to Carson City. For a man like Clint, who was used to traveling at Eclipse's pace, the state line didn't seem nearly as far away. Dover Shallows had been a ways off from the Nevada border, but thanks to a bit of backtracking to get to Johnny's wagon, Clint figured on arriving at Carson City after making camp only twice.

The first night was quiet. Rosa ate a few bites of the food Clint offered and went to sleep. She didn't complain about the ropes tied around her or the fact that she was tethered to a tree like a dog. After a second day of hard riding, Clint made camp and took the time to prepare something other than fried oats and bacon.

A freshly killed rabbit hung on a spit over a fire, and a nearby stream provided fresh water for his canteen. Biting into the rabbit stew Clint pulled together was enough to bring a smile to Rosa's face.

"This is really good," she said.

Clint laughed and said, "Wait until I kill a possum. Then you'll really be in for a treat."

". . . want to thank you."

"For what? Catching you, tying you up, or hauling you to a jail?"

"None of those, so much, but I should thank you for getting me away from Franco. He would have killed me rather than let me go. I'm sure of that."

Scooping up some of the stew, Clint nodded. "Well, no need to worry about that anymore."

"I know," she said with a relieved sigh. "Thank you."

Clint kept eating, and waited for her to ask him to loosen the ropes or maybe even let her go stretch her legs. None of those requests came, though. In fact, she didn't say much of anything until she was finished with her supper.

"All this riding must make you tired," she said after Clint took her plate.

"Don't worry about me. I'll be fine."

"I wish I could wash off some of this dirt."

Nodding as he finally heard the type of thing he'd been waiting for, Clint asked, "I suppose you'd like me to let you have some time in the river so you could refresh yourself?"

"Yes. That would be nice."

"How about I lead you down there and I'll wash off these plates? Or I could just save you some time, find a nice heavy rock, and hit myself over the back of the head with it. At least that way you wouldn't even need to get your hands dirty."

"I wasn't thinking about that," Rosa said. She grinned and cocked her head. "But that isn't a bad idea."

"Just save all the sweet talk," Clint said. "I intend on bringing you to the jail and that's that. You're pretty, but not so pretty that I'll let my guard down every time you bat your eyelids."

"Could you maybe bring me some water so I could wash a little of this dirt from my hair?" When she asked that question, Rosa sifted her fingers through her hair and caused a good amount of dirt and silt to billow around her head like a cloud.

"I'm not loosening your ropes," Clint told her.

"I didn't expect you to."

Knowing that he'd arranged the entire camp with the length of her ropes in mind, Clint thought about what she might be trying to accomplish by getting him to bring her water. Although he was unable to think of anything beyond her obvious desire to get free, Clint looked at Rosa as if he could see right through her.

"I'm going to search you before I take one step from here," he said. "Actually, I'm going to search you anyway."

Clint walked over to her with his hand clasped over his holstered Colt. The closer he got to her, the wider Rosa's smile became.

"What's so funny?" Clint asked.

"I was just wondering how many guns you think I found between now and the last time you searched me. Or maybe you think I pulled a knife out of that old horse I'm riding?"

"That's enough."

But it was too late for Rosa to stop. She was laughing at him more the longer she talked, until she was too far gone to rein it in. "And I guess you think I've got some good places to hide this arsenal I found? Is that how a man's mind works?"

"I'm still going to search you."

The longer she seemed to be distracting him, the more Clint expected her to make her move. When she finally broke into a full belly laugh, he drew his pistol just to put an end to the noise.

Not only did it cause her to stop laughing, but it made him feel like a genuine horse's ass in the process.

Lowering his Colt and keeping his hand over the grip like before, he said, "Sorry about that. I just . . ."

"I know," she said earnestly. "If only we'd met under better circumstances."

"Yeah. If only."

She raised her arms and extended her legs. "Go ahead and search. I don't blame you for not trusting me."

Clint repeated the same process as he'd done before, searching her from her head to her toes without stepping out of line as to where he put his hands. Rosa was still laughing a bit and even squirmed when his hands got too close to her hips or under her arms.

"That tickled," she explained.

When he'd taken her prisoner, Clint's notion of her was fixed solidly in his mind. But the more time he spent with Rosa and the more he thought about what he actually knew of her, the more he started to wonder if he hadn't been too quick to judge her.

He was taking her to jail. That wasn't going to change.

He hadn't let his guard down once. That wouldn't change either.

But there was no reason she shouldn't be allowed to clean up a bit.

"I'll be right back with some water," he said.

TWENTY

After cleaning out the stewpot, Clint filled it with river water and brought it back to the camp. He'd barely let Rosa out of his sight the entire time he'd been gone, and the river was less than twenty paces from the tree where she was tied. Even so, he was hesitant as he approached her again.

Clint set the pot down and took a good look at her. As far as he could tell, Rosa hadn't moved from the spot she'd been in when he left to go to the river. She still sat in a patch of grass with her legs curled up beneath her. She looked back at him with an almost bored expression on her face as her hands idly plucked blades of grass from the ground.

The night was young enough for a few streaks of light to show in the sky. It was the time of day when everything was bathed in a warm, red glow. A few of the brighter stars could already be seen in the eastern half of the horizon.

Clint approached her carefully with his hand resting upon the grip of his holstered Colt. He went through the motions of searching her again and found nothing on her that hadn't been there before. By the time he was done, he shrugged and said, "You're still clean."

"Not really," she said. "But I will be as soon as I get some of that water."

Clint stepped back and pushed the stewpot toward her. As Rosa dipped her hands into the water, Clint made preparations so they could leave as quickly as possible in the morning. He packed away everything they wouldn't need in the meantime, which meant he only left out his bedroll and the fixings for tomorrow's breakfast.

All the while, Clint made sure to keep Rosa in his field of vision. He may not have been watching her like a hawk, but he was able to see enough to know she wasn't doing anything she wasn't supposed to be doing. When he heard the sounds of splashing water come to a stop, he looked over at her.

Rosa was on her knees with her back straight. Her long brown hair was just wet enough to stay together in the breeze as it fell over one shoulder. The rest of the water had been used on her body, causing her white shirt to cling to her like a second skin, allowing Clint to see the dark shape of her nipples poking from behind the moist cotton.

Her hands ran along the edge of the stewpot and then slowly eased it forward. Pulling in a deep breath, she parted her lips for a moment before saying, "You can take this back now."

Clint walked forward and kept his eyes fixed on her. Part of him was waiting for her to make a move against him, but another part simply couldn't look away. "You want something to dry off?"

She shook her head. As Clint took the stewpot away, she asked, "Aren't you going to search me again?"

"Maybe later."

"I don't think I can wait any longer."

Clint was putting the stewpot away and had his back to her. He could feel his body reacting to the sultry tone in her voice. That, combined with the sight of her in those dripping wet clothes, made it difficult for him to keep his mind on track. Thinking about what could happen if he took a misstep was enough to get him more or less where he needed to be.

Turning around, Clint said, "I know what you're trying to do. I'm not an idiot."

"I told you before that I'm not a killer. Tell me one lie you caught me in and I'll understand why you think I'd hurt you."

"Lying isn't a part of it. You riding with an assassin is more than enough for me to be wary of you."

"I'm not the one who wanted to kill you. Besides," she said as she stood up and peeled off her jeans, "you can see for yourself I'm unarmed."

Clint was able to keep his expression neutral as Rosa kicked off her wet jeans so they landed next to her boots. That only left her button-up shirt, which was just large enough to cover her. No matter how well he maintained his composure, Rosa kept right on pushing him to his limit.

She kept her eyes on Clint while opening her shirt one button at a time. Once all the buttons were undone, she held open the shirt as if she were holding open a jacket to show she wasn't heeled. "See?" she said while doing a slow turn. "You've got nothing to worry about."

Having already looked at her closely to see if she posed a threat, Clint now looked at her just to let his eyes soak in the sight of her. Beads of water ran down her light brown skin. Her body moved sensually even when she was lowering herself to the ground and sitting with her legs slightly parted.

"Franco only slept with me because he said it made his eyes sharper," she told him. "I want you to make love to me as a man should make love to a woman. It may be a long time before I feel such a thing again."

Clint knew he should turn his back to her and walk over to his own bedroll. But the longer he thought about how much he shouldn't go to her, the more he wanted to.

"Aw hell," Clint muttered as he unbuckled his holster and tossed it to where Eclipse was standing.

TWENTY-ONE

By the time Clint stepped within Rosa's reach, he was only wearing his boots and jeans. Everything else had been tossed into a pile behind him. Rosa was once again on her knees, waiting for him. Her eyes were wide as if she couldn't believe he was actually coming to her. She breathed in quick, expectant gasps.

Rosa's legs had been untied so she could move around a bit, but her wrists were still bound together and a rope attached them to a nearby tree. She'd gotten better at moving around the ropes and didn't even seem to notice them until she reached out to pull on Clint's belt.

"I'm not untying you," he said.

"Just come a little closer," she replied breathlessly.

Clint stood his ground and said, "Lay down."

She seemed surprised at first, but in a way that only fed the excitement burning in her eyes. Quickly, Rosa did as she was told by getting onto all fours and then rolling onto her back. When she looked up for Clint, she found him already coming down to her. Rosa sat up and spread her legs open wide.

The moment Rosa reached out to touch his face, Clint's first instinct was to grab hold of her wrists so she couldn't do any damage. Rosa reacted with a quick intake of breath. Her eyes got an even hungrier look in them, and her nipples became hard beneath the wet cotton shirt.

Clint had reacted so quickly that he didn't have a chance to think. Now that he had ahold of the ropes tying her wrists together, he tightened his grip and slid his other hand under her shirt. Rosa reacted immediately by arching her back and leaning her head back as Clint's hand explored her breasts.

Rosa's body was soft and tense at the same time. Her skin was smooth, but her muscles quivered beneath his hand. Once he cupped her breast and massaged it, Clint could feel her relaxing and letting out a slow breath.

Holding her arms up a bit, Clint leaned forward to run his tongue between her breasts while teasing her nipple with his thumb. Rosa didn't put up one bit of struggle. In fact, she wriggled and squirmed as a way to guide his lips to where she wanted them to go.

Once Clint started nibbling at a spot on her neck, she pressed herself against him and urgently whispered, "Right there. Oh my God, that's so good."

Even though Clint had ahold of her wrists, he quickly realized that she had ahold of him in another way. Rosa's legs wrapped around his waist, drawing him in closer until she was grinding herself against his rigid cock.

Clint looked down to watch the way she moved. By the time he slowly ran his hand along the side of her body, she'd positioned herself so the tip of his penis was nestled between the lips of her pussy. Her eyes were closed and her hair was tossed behind her as she began thrusting her hips forward until he was finally inside of her.

After allowing her to slide her wet lips along the length of his cock a few times, Clint leaned forward and pushed her onto the ground. Rosa landed solidly and snapped her eyes open. Her smile was wider than ever, and her mouth hung open as if she was about to say something. Those words didn't come out before she felt him straighten out her arms over her head by tugging the rope a little tighter.

"Oh . . . oh, yes!" she moaned. As Clint slid all the way inside of her, she arched her back and repeated herself again and again.

One of Rosa's legs was looped around him and the other was braced against the ground. The cotton shirt lay open beneath her, making the color of her skin stand out like she was laying on a bed of spilled cream.

Even though she appeared to struggle against his hold on the ropes, Rosa never made a serious attempt to break Clint's grip. As he pumped his hips between her legs, Clint was still waiting for her to try to take advantage of a moment or gain an upper hand. Just then, however, Rosa was more than content to let him be in control.

Soon, Rosa did make a move that Clint wasn't expecting. It wasn't exactly an unwelcome one, either.

The first thing Clint felt was her pulling against the ropes binding her wrists. Clint's free hand had reached around to cup her buttocks and lift her up a bit as he thrust forward. When he felt her struggling, Clint stopped and looked to see what she had in mind.

Rosa's breaths were coming in loud gasps. She looked at him and winked while wriggling on the ground to give herself some slack in the ropes. Clint allowed her to go, just to see what she was up to. Before long, Rosa was able to bend her elbows and sit upright.

"What are you doing?" Clint asked.

She kept scooting toward the tree and then got onto all fours so she could crawl to it. "I just want a little more rope to work with," she said.

Although Clint was wary of her intentions, he enjoyed watching her crawl toward the tree where the rope was tied. Her legs dragged through the grass and her backside twitched slowly back and forth. Following her, Clint stopped before she could get close enough to the tree to grab a low-hanging branch. He no longer held her by the wrists, but he kept hold of the rope.

"That's far enough," he warned. "Maybe this isn't such a good . . ."

His words trailed off as Clint saw Rosa lean forward and dig her fingers into the ground like a cat stretching its back. Her backside was raised even higher and she looked over her shoulder with lust smoldering in her eyes.

"This is just right," she said. "Come and see for yourself."

Clint settled in behind her and rubbed his free hand along the curve of her buttocks. After wrapping the rope around his other hand, he had just enough slack to drape the rope over her back while she kept her hands pressed flat against the ground in front of her. The tree wasn't far in front, but there was nothing for her to reach and no branch anywhere close to Rosa's grasp.

When Clint brushed the rope against her back, Rosa flinched and let out a slow moan. He rubbed her backside, savoring the way her tight muscles and smooth skin felt under his hand. He even gave her a little slap on the hip, which caused Rosa to moan louder and lift her backside higher.

By now, Clint was so hard that he would start to ache if he didn't get inside of her. He guided his cock to her waiting pussy and pushed his hips forward. She was so wet that he glided in easily. Her moist lips wrapped around him and even tightened a bit as he lingered inside of her.

"Don't make me wait for it," she moaned. "Please."

Clint tugged on the rope as he eased out and thrust his hips forward. This time, he didn't hesitate or prolong the moment in the least. He pumped into her again and again until she was gritting her teeth and groaning as an orgasm pulsed through her body.

Clint could feel her climaxing as her muscles twitched and she rocked against him with every thrust. Soon, Rosa brought her head up and flung her hair along her back as she gazed up at the darkening sky. She bit down on her lower lip and trembled as one orgasm fed into another.

As his own climax approached, Clint almost let the rope slip from his hand. Not only did Rosa not try to use that momentary weakness against him, but she didn't even seem to notice it. She was too busy reeling with the intense pleasure she was feeling, and Clint was about to join her.

A few more powerful thrusts and Clint exploded inside of her. By the time he was finished, Rosa's legs were almost too weak to support her own weight.

Reluctantly, Clint got up. "I . . . still can't untie you," he said.

It took a few seconds for her to catch her breath. When she did, Rosa replied, "After this . . . I actually don't mind these ropes anymore."

TWENTY-TWO

Tom Clark was a barrel-chested man with a grizzled face and stubbly, gray hair. His fingers were like thick sausages, and when he took hold of the reins to Rosa's horse, he clamped around the leather straps like a vise.

"This little lady did all that?" Tom asked after Clint was finished explaining why he was handing Rosa into his custody.

"She was the lookout for Franco Dominguez when he intended on picking off me and my friend in Dover Shallows," Clint explained. "I'm pretty sure she was there when we got ambushed, but I didn't see her fire a shot."

"Just acting as a lookout again, huh?"

"That's my guess."

Tom looked up to Rosa with calculating eyes. Although he took a second to appreciate her figure, he didn't let his eyes linger on her for too long. "Pretty ones like this tend to favor the troublemakers," Tom muttered. "They also tend to think their pretty faces will get 'em out of whatever trouble they get into."

"That's why I handed her over to you, Tom. Only a happily married man like yourself could resist such feminine wiles."

Tom looked over to Clint's smirking face and let out a choppy laugh. "Shit, you're just saying that because you met my wife. You know damn well she'd skin me alive if she thought I laid a finger on a young little thing like this one."

"There's that, too."

"I've got some men riding not too far from Dover Shallows. I can send word to them and have them check in with the local law over there. If need be, can I count on you to testify to what you saw?"

"Sure," Clint replied with a nod. "If I'm not here, you can send a telegram to Rick Hartman. You remember him?"

"It'd be hard to forget Rick's Place! I had some of the best meatloaf in my life over there!"

"I'll be sure to let Mrs. Clark know about that."

Clearing his throat and shifting on his feet, Tom said, "When'd you say you were leaving Carson City?"

"Just as soon as you buy me a beer. I tend to lose track of what I was going to say after I've had one or two."

"Then I'll buy you three! As far as you know, my wife's cookin' is the best there is!"

Clint laughed as he watched a younger marshal lead Rosa away. She sat warily in the saddle, but that was mostly because she hadn't been able to shift to a better position throughout the entire ride. Even so, she managed to smile back at him.

"She give you any trouble?" Tom asked once her horse had been led far enough away so she couldn't overhear them.

"Actually, no."

"You seem surprised by that."

Clint let out a sigh and nodded slowly. "I am. Both the times my friend and I crossed that assassin's path, she wasn't anywhere to be found. I'm pretty sure I spotted her at that first ambush, but that was at a distance."

"The lookout," Tom said. "You mentioned that."

"Still, she admitted to as much when I asked her about it, and she was more than willing to answer my questions about who put Dominguez on our tails."

"Care to share that information?"

"I was going to follow up on that myself."

"I trust you to keep it legal, Clint. Far as I'm concerned, you're justified to pay this asshole a visit without crossing the line."

"I think I can manage that," Clint said.

"If there's anything I can do to help, you just need to ask."

"Is there a way you could check on a man by the name of Galloway who works for Western Union?"

"How much do you need to know?"

"Just where he is."

Tom shrugged. "Shouldn't be too hard. Those fellas usually ain't too far from a telegraph wire." Draping an arm around Clint, Tom asked, "You sure there ain't more to tell me about this lady? As of now, there's not a lot to throw at her."

"To be honest, I don't know if there should be more charges against her. I told you everything I know and don't have any reason to know any more."

"What about this assassin? I've heard of a man looking like the one you described at a few killings, but that's about it."

"Actually, there is something else." With that, Clint reached behind him to remove Franco's .44 from under his gun belt. Holding it flat in his hand, Clint showed it to the marshal and explained, "This was his gun. I've had a chance to look it over and it's more than just a pretty, expensive piece."

Tom let out a slow whistle. "A gun like that would go a long way to fund my retirement."

"Which is another reason why I'm handing it over to

you instead of someone who might actually make good on a notion like that."

Sighing as if cursing his own conscience, Tom asked, "What else is there to that pistol?"

"Apart from the sapphire and engravings, it's been modified to be quicker on the draw and deliver a harder punch than most .44s. It's not quite enough of a change to make it a different caliber, but it would definitely fire a bit farther than a standard gun like this."

"Ain't nothing standard about that," Tom said.

"Exactly. It's even got a better than average chance of shooting through things that might stop a regular round. If I would've known that, I would have been a little more careful going against him."

Tom shook his head and patted Clint's shoulder. "Skill will trump firepower any day of the week, my friend."

"And a bit of luck doesn't hurt." With that, Clint handed over the pistol.

"I can ask around to see if anyone else has seen someone carrying a gun like this. That might be enough to tie this Dominguez and maybe even his lady over there to another killing or two."

Even though that same thing had been on Clint's mind, he wasn't anxious to heap more trouble onto Rosa's back. He was also quick to remind himself that if Tom Clark connected her to more deaths, then she deserved whatever trouble came her way.

"I'm going to get a room for the night and some real food in my belly," Clint said. "And don't think I'll let you off the hook where those beers are concerned."

"Wouldn't dream of it," Tom said. "My wife's gonna insist you come over for dinner, as well. Ducking her ain't too wise."

"I'll stay on an extra day for some home cooking."

"Then it's settled. I believe there's a card game or two to be had at the Blaylock Saloon. That should keep you busy until I meet you there. We can have some beers and swap stories."

Clint tipped his hat to the marshal and started to walk away. The younger lawman was cutting Rosa's ropes and helping her down from the horse. Knowing she was in good hands, Clint led Eclipse to the closest stable.

TWENTY-THREE

The Blaylock was a small saloon that not a lot of people knew about. Fortunately for the saloon's owners, enough poker players preferred their tables over the others in Carson City for them to keep the place open for business. It also served good enough food to keep Clint there for the entire night after he checked into his room.

After a hearty meal, Clint sat in on a friendly game until he saw Tom Clark walk through the front door. U.S. Marshal Clark tossed a wave in Clint's direction, found his way to the bar, and ordered two beers. By the time Clint stepped up beside him, Tom had already drained over half of his first mug.

"Any luck?" Tom asked.

Clint patted his pocket and replied, "Enough that I needed to cash out rather than pay up."

"You been cheating the locals again?"

"Buy some chips and see for yourself."

"I may look stupid, but I know better than to sit across a card table from you. Been waiting long?"

"Not long enough for me to lose interest."

Tom laughed and pushed a full mug of beer to Clint. "And aren't you in high spirits all of a sudden?"

"It feels good knowing that I'll have a mattress under me tonight."

"And something soft and warm on top of you, if I'm guessing correctly."

"Just sleep will be fine for tonight."

Shrugging, Tom finished his beer and slapped the bar for another. "I hate to knock the grin off yer face, but I already heard back about that gun you handed over."

"And?"

"And a few other marshals in New Mex recognized it the moment I brought up the sapphire in the handle."

"What about the man who carried it?" Clint asked.

"They said something about a Mexican fella, but he could have also been a Spaniard. My gut tells me he could have also been Chinese for all they know. They seemed a hell of a lot clearer about the gun."

"That figures. So that means Dominguez was either real good at keeping his head down or there's more than one person using that gun."

"Or one just like it," Tom added.

"I thought about that, too. Actually, I was trying not to think about it."

The marshal shrugged his shoulders. "Sounds to me like you handled that Spanish fella well enough."

"I got lucky once or twice," Clint said as he thought back to the first shot that had been fired when Franco ambushed him and Johnny while on the trail. "If there is some sort of organization of assassins at work here, it's going to take a lot more luck than anyone has to get through them all."

"And what makes you think they'd throw all they got at you?" Tom winced and added, "Maybe I should put that another way."

"Point taken," Clint said. "Did you find out anything else?"

"I sure did! Galloway's still right where you left him. I

just sent a wire to the spot you mentioned before and got an answer right quick."

Clint nodded and took another drink of his beer. The brew was a good balance that left a nice flavor in his mouth while also having enough alcohol in it to calm his nerves. "Then I'll be heading back that way. If he hired that assassin to come after me and Johnny, that makes him just as guilty as the one who pulled the trigger."

"More guilty if you ask me," Tom grumbled.

"You think so?"

"Hell yes! A real assassin, not just a killer but a real professional, don't kill nobody unless he gets paid for it."

"An assassin is a killer, the last time I checked."

"Sure, and a real good one. Most killers are mean-spirited, wicked souls, or just plain foul drunks. They're dangerous because they're bound to go off and hurt anyone around them when they do. That's the sort of person paying the money to an assassin. They've got all the bad intent behind what they're doing, but just don't have the guts to pull the trigger.

"The assassin may be a killer, but he's really no worse than the gun he holds," Tom said, while making the shape of a pistol with his thumb and forefinger. "He'll sit nice and quiet without harming a soul. He'll go to church and live a long time without making a fuss. If nobody hires him for long enough, he'll find some other line of work. Once that asshole with the money steps up . . ." To cap off his own sentence, Tom dropped his thumb as the hammer of his make-believe pistol.

Clint laughed and leaned against the bar. "No worse than the gun he holds, huh? In this case, that's saying a lot."

"Sure enough. That's one hell of a gun."

TWENTY-FOUR

A few days passed, and Clint spent the first of them social-izing with the Clarks. He had some more beers with Tom, played cards at the Blaylock Saloon, and ate dinner with the marshal and his wife. Once that was done, Clint sad-dled up Eclipse and rode out of Carson City to retrace his steps west to where he'd met up with Johnny Blevin.

As those same days passed, Johnny bought a ticket on a ship bound for Wales, with a carriage meant to drive him all the way into London. He left from a small port that didn't bat an eye at the fake name they were given. Johnny spent his time trading off between savoring his newly found wealth and looking over his shoulder for someone carrying a sapphire gun.

The passage of those days hit Rosa especially hard, since she spent them in a jail cell. Tom and his men treated her just fine, but the walls were thick enough to keep the sights and sounds of the outside world away from her. The food was terrible, the water was dirty, and she had nothing to do but pace, sit and sleep.

She was surprised at the way the marshals treated her. After the first two days passed and she had nothing but boredom to complain about, Rosa figured the lawmen hadn't found out the extent of the kills Franco had made. Compared to how she'd expected to be treated, these jailers were downright cordial.

The marshal who'd brought her in at the start was the one who'd searched her upon locking her up. His hands had been quick and thoroughly efficient, which was a poor comparison in her mind to the searches Clint had given her. After that first search, the marshal had tossed a plain gray dress into her cell and told her to toss her old clothes out.

He stood there and watched as she stripped down and fit the new dress over her head. Actually, the new garment was only a dress by the loosest definition of the word. It was more like a sack with three holes at the top for her head and arms to slip through.

Every day, Rosa expected something more from the marshals. She expected to see Tom Clark walk in and confront her about the grisly details regarding the deputies Franco had killed a few months ago. She knew she'd catch hell for the federals that were killed once they tried to chase her and Franco down after they assassinated that lance corporal in Fort Sanders.

In fact, the most trouble she'd gotten was from the two other prisoners that had been locked in neighboring cells. One of them was a rowdy asshole with crooked teeth and bruises on his face from the guff he'd given to Tom Clark while being brought in. He bragged about the hell he'd raised, but Rosa had him pegged as nothing more than a big talker.

The other prisoner was a quiet black man who'd been captured after a store owner accused him of stealing. He'd been brought in one night and shoved into his cell without him saying a word. Soon after that, one of the other marshals came by to let the man know he'd be released as soon as they could convince the shopkeeper to drop the charges. It seemed even the law was aware of the accuser's tendency to suspect a man of color rather than his own son, who'd been caught stealing from his father's store several times before.

For the most part, the marshals only looked in on Rosa from time to time to give her food, water, or to dump the pot that sat in the corner of each cell. There wasn't much need for them to watch over the prisoners every moment of the day, since each cell was basically a solid box of thick iron bars in a room locked by a door that could possibly withstand a battering ram. Her window was just big enough for her to crawl through if it, too, hadn't been sealed off by thick iron bars.

What surprised her more than anything else was that the marshals let her keep her boots. Perhaps Tom was confident since Clint had had custody of her for so long beforehand. Perhaps the marshals were lazy, or even out of boots for women. Whichever it was, Rosa was thankful. Once she heard the tap of something against the bars of her window, she was doubly grateful.

The loudmouth was currently asleep, and the black man lay stretched out on his cot as always.

"You awake in there?" came a voice from the outside world.

Rosa jumped up from her cot and rushed to the window. It was just high enough to prevent her from looking out to see much of anything apart from a sliver of sky. At the moment, that sky was pitch-black. "I'm awake. Is that you, Mackie?"

She may not have been able to see much of anything through the window, but she recognized the thick fingers snaking their way through the bars. "You got that right. Is that marshal in there with you?"

"No."

"Then he must still be in his office. What about anyone else?"

"Two others," she whispered.

Rosa couldn't contain herself any longer. She pulled the

cot beneath the window, hopped onto it, and stood on her tiptoes to get a better look through the window. "I think the other two in here are asleep, but they're in different cells."

Wes Mackie was a big enough man that he already looked to be at the same height as Rosa while she was standing on her cot. Long, stringy dark hair hung over most of his face. Another sizable chunk of his face was covered by a full, scruffy beard. He smiled at her the moment he saw her face.

"Still pretty as ever," he said.

"You should see this dress they gave me."

"You still got them boots that I like so much?"

She smirked and nodded. "Yes, I do."

"Then you might be able to help me out." Mackie glanced over his shoulder at the space behind him. When he looked back again, he lifted something in one hand that Rosa couldn't see until he slipped it between the bars. It was an iron hook connected to a chain, which rattled against the outside of the wall.

"Just give me a minute to get ready and then let me know when you're ready to go," he said. "You think you can take the guard or should I do it?"

"I will," Rosa said quickly. "Just do whatever you got to do."

TWENTY-FIVE

The jail was a brick building directly behind the U.S. Marshals' office. It was so close to the office that it was practically connected to the bigger building and had a small walkway running between the two.

Looking through the window, Rosa was surprised just how much of the day had gotten away from her. The last time she'd checked, there was still sunlight coming through her window. Now it looked as if it was the middle of the night.

The only thing in the lot behind the jail was a set of outhouses used by the marshals and prisoners, alike. After squinting into the shadows for a few seconds, she could just make out the chain, which ran away from the wall and behind the outhouses. Soon, she spotted several large shapes moving closer to the rectangular shacks. One of them was Mackie, and the others were horses he led to the opposite end of the chain.

Before the horses could get too close, Rosa hopped down from her cot and rushed to her bars. Kicking and pounding on them with all of her strength, she soon realized she was barely making any noise. Without missing a beat, she rushed to her chamber pot and smacked it against the iron bars.

"Will you shut the fuck up?" the asshole in the other cell shouted as he sat up. "I am trying to sleep, you fucking nigger!"

The black man in the cell next to him shifted to look at him with an intense glare. Once he had the asshole's attention, he pointed a finger over to Rosa.

Seeing what she was doing, the asshole grunted, "What the fuck is your problem, bitch?"

After looking to see that there was still a bit of fluid at the bottom of the pot, she reared back and tossed it through the bars toward the asshole's cell. Even though no more than a light spray made it between cells, the asshole hollered as if he'd been caught in the face with a bucket of acid.

"God damn you! Throwing piss on me! I'll kill you, bitch!"

Rosa smiled as the asshole shouted louder and louder. She added to the ruckus by pulling in a breath and cutting loose with a piercing scream that nearly rattled every iron bar in the jail.

Before too much more of that, the front door of the jail swung open and one of the marshals stormed inside. It was the same marshal who'd brought Rosa into her cell and made sure she was comfortable ever since. He was a younger guy with a solid build, and he rushed inside with a shotgun in his hands.

"What in the hell is going on in here?" the marshal shouted. The first place his eyes were drawn was to the asshole in the cell to his left. "Can't you even stay in a cage without stirring up a shit storm?"

"She threw piss at me!" the asshole snapped back as he stuck an arm through the bars to point at Rosa.

The instant that arm came through the bars, the marshal

aimed his shotgun at the asshole's cell. "You make one move toward me and I'll shut you up for good."

Pulling back his arm and then stepping away from the bars, the asshole said, "I wasn't moving against you. I was just telling you that bitch is the one who started all of this."

The marshal put his back to the door and kept his shotgun close to him. The cell farthest from him was occupied by the black man, who also happened to be the quietest person in the jail. To the marshal's right, Rosa stood innocently in her cell. The frightened expression on her face seemed even odder when compared to the mess in her cell.

"What have you been doing in there?" the marshal asked Rosa. "Why's there such a mess?"

"He did it," she replied while nodding toward the asshole.

"What?" Even as that word was coming out of the marshal's mouth, he was reaching out to check the door of the asshole's cell. It was still locked, so the marshal checked the black man's door as well. Finding that to be locked, he backed toward Rosa. "What did he do?"

"He tried to come into my cell and rape me," Rosa said in a shaky voice.

The asshole let out a few sputtering words that sounded more like he was throwing up. Finally, he spat out, "That's bullshit! My damn door is locked!"

"It is now!" Rosa shouted. "You were just over here, throwing me off my cot and storming around here saying you wanted to bend me over and stick your little pencil dick inside of me."

"What?! I didn't . . . it's not . . . !"

"Shut up," the marshal hollered. "Both of you!" The lawman stepped over to Rosa's cell and tried her door, only to find that it was locked just as solidly as the others. Turning toward the two men, he said, "I don't know what the hell you think you're doing, but if you don't quiet down and clean up this goddamn mess, I'll come back in here with—"

Suddenly, Rosa's left arm shot through the bars and grabbed hold of the marshal's neck. The moment she had her wrist cinched in under his chin, she pulled him toward her so the back of his head knocked against the bars of her cell. Her right arm shot out as well, crossed over his neck, and snapped across his throat.

The movements happened so quickly that they took all three men by surprise. Before any of them knew what was happening, blood sprayed from the marshal's neck and he let out a gurgling wheeze.

Before the marshal could even think about firing his shotgun, Rosa's arm snapped down again and blood flew from the vein on the inside of his elbow. The marshal's arm went limp, allowing the shotgun to drop, but he was too busy dying to notice.

Reaching up with his other hand, the marshal felt the gaping wound in his neck. His eyes looked around wildly without seeing a thing. His mouth moved as if to form words, but only more gurgles came out. Blood poured through his fingers and seeped into his shirt. After the marshal dropped against the cell door, the other two prisoners could see Rosa standing directly behind him.

TWENTY-SIX

The knife in Rosa's hand was so thin that it was hard to see. Its blade had a slight curve to it, as though it had been specifically crafted to slit throats. Rosa looked over at the other two prisoners as if she was ready to charge straight through anything in her way just to get at them.

Still too scared to say anything to her, the asshole held up both hands and backed away from his bars.

The black man in the cell next to him, however, had gotten up and was grabbing hold of the bars so he could get a better look at Rosa.

She dropped to one knee and slipped the knife back into the scabbard stitched into the side of her boot. The slender compartment didn't stand out in the slightest from the other stitching in the plain boots, which came midway up her calf. Once the knife was sheathed, only the handle could be seen. It was flat as a nail file and almost as skinny. Embedded in the handle was a single, small sapphire.

"If you two keep quiet and watch the door, I'll let you out of here," she said while fitting the small hook sewn into the flap of her boot into its corresponding eye. When she took her hand away, the knife and its sheath had disappeared into the side of her boot.

The black man leaned against his bars and said, "I can do you some good, lady. Take me with you."

"You don't even know where I'm going," she said as she reached through the bars to fish in the dead marshal's pockets.

"It don't matter. Just so long as it's away from here."

Before too long, Rosa found what she was looking for and held the ring of keys out so she could start fitting them into her lock one at a time.

"Me too," the asshole grunted. "I got friends all over this county. Family too! They'll hide us, feed us, you name it!"

Rosa knew she'd found the key she'd been after when it turned in the lock and her door came open. The first thing she did was grab the marshal's shotgun and rush to the door of the jailhouse. Once she'd taken a quick peek outside, she headed back to her cell and reached up to loosen the hook around the bar in her window.

After the hook had thumped to the ground, Mackie's voice drifted in from the outside. "You all right?"

"Fine," Rosa replied. "Just get the horses ready so we can go. I've arranged a quieter exit for us."

"Sounds good to me."

"Sounds good to me, too," the asshole grunted. "We gettin' out of here now, or what?"

Rosa nodded and then turned toward the black man's cell. "What's your name?" she asked.

"Eli Washington."

"Here you go, Eli," she said while tossing the keys to him. "Be quick about it."

Catching the keys effortlessly, Eli immediately tried one after the other until his door swung open as well. Once he stepped out, he found himself at the wrong end of Rosa's shotgun.

"Can I trust you, Eli?"

"Yes, ma'am. I'd rather ride along with you and whoever's out there than take my chances with a judge that'd rather hang me than embarrass some shop owner's kid."

"You'll need to prove yourself."

"I will, ma'am." Looking over to the asshole, who now had both arms sticking through the bars with hands open, Eli asked, "Is he coming along with us?"

"That's up to you."

As Eli approached the cell, the asshole grinned at him from behind the bars.

"No hard feelings about what I said before," the asshole said. "Hand over them keys and you'll be treated like my own brother."

Eli stepped in front of the cell, still holding the keys in his hand at his side. When he began lifting that hand, the asshole reached through the bars to try and snag the keys for himself. Eli's grip remained solid, and rather than let the asshole take the keys, he pulled the greedy hand even farther through the bars.

"What the hell?" the asshole gasped in surprise.

Having let go of the keys so both hands were now free, Eli got hold of both the asshole's arms and pulled again. This time, he pulled so hard that the asshole's face slammed against the bars with a muted thump.

The asshole's chin was wedged between two iron bars, and his nose was bent at an odd angle. Just as he was about to say something, the asshole was pushed back and pulled forward with even more force. His nose cracked and his jaw crunched slightly out of its socket. The third time he was slammed against the bars was enough to knock him out. After the fourth and fifth, his arms were dislocated and his face was lost beneath a messy red paste.

Eli let go and watched as the asshole dropped to the floor. Sweat was forming on his brow, and he used the back of his hand to wipe it away as he turned around to get a look at Rosa.

For a moment, Rosa seemed almost as surprised as the asshole had been. In fact, she still held her shotgun aimed at the dead man's cell, as if there was a need for her to pull the trigger. Lowering the shotgun, she said, "You made the right choice. I sure as hell wasn't taking that prick with me."

"And he won't say nothing to nobody," Eli added. "Does that count as proving myself?"

"It gets you a ticket out of town with me and my friend. How's that?"

"Good enough, ma'am."

"Call me Rosa. And this," she said while stepping outside and pointing to the big fellow holding the reins to four horses, "is Mackie."

"He's coming with us?" Mackie asked.

"Yes," Rosa said. "I'll explain once we're out of here. Scout ahead and make sure the way's clear. We're right behind you."

She and Eli each chose a horse and climbed onto its back. The fourth had the length of chain wrapped around its shoulders like a steel harness.

Mackie brought his horse around and rode toward the front of the Marshals' office. He snapped his reins and got his horse moving down the street.

As soon as Mackie rode by, a man crossed the street and turned to watch him go. Just then, Rosa and Eli rode out from behind the Marshals' office. The man stopped and fixed his eyes on them.

Rosa recognized Tom Clark's face almost as quickly as he recognized hers.

As his hand went for the pistol at his side, Tom asked, "What're you doin' out of—"

He was cut short by the roar of the shotgun Rosa had taken from the younger marshal. The buckshot hit Tom square in the chest and even broke the window of the shop behind him as he fell backward against the dark building.

His hand had made it to his pistol, but he didn't have the strength to lift it.

Tom didn't even have enough life left in him to watch as Rosa and Eli rode away.

TWENTY-SEVEN

They stuck to the main roads as much as possible. With the moon reduced to nothing more than a sliver in the sky, staying on any road was a challenge. Once they were far enough outside of Carson City, however, Mackie lit some torches, passed them out, and kept on riding.

After an hour, they left the road and took another well-known route to a watering hole favored by travelers. From there, they rode a little ways more, until they found a spot where they could stop and catch a breath without being seen.

"Is this far enough away to be safe?" Rosa asked without climbing down from her horse. "If we need to ride more, we should do that."

"We're lucky we made it this far in the middle of the night," Mackie replied. "You wanna push your luck some more?"

Eli raised his voice just loud enough to be heard. "He's right, ma'am. It's dangerous to ride so fast this late at night."

Twisting around in her saddle to look at Eli, Rosa snapped, "Shut up! You're lucky to be alive and out of that damn cage."

Anger flared in Eli's eyes, but he kept it under control. Seeing how Mackie was tensed and ready to back Rosa's play made that feat quite a bit easier.

Rosa turned to look once more at her partner. "Once those dead lawmen are found, the rest will be coming after us."

"There was only one in there when I checked," Mackie said.

"There was another that you rode straight past on your way out of town."

"And you killed him? Jesus! That gunshot came from you?"

"He looked right at me! He knew who I was. What the hell else was I supposed to do?"

"That how it happened?" Mackie asked as he glanced over to Eli.

The black man nodded once. Apparently, it was an earnest enough nod for Mackie to believe it.

Even though he believed it, Mackie wasn't happy about it. "Shit," he muttered. "That's just great."

"Like two dead marshals is much worse than one," Rosa said. "Either way, they'll be after us. For all we know, they could be tracking us down right now."

Mackie shook his head. "It's too dark for them to see shit. Anyhow, this road is traveled so much that any trace we left behind will just mix in with whatever was left behind by all the others who've ridden on it."

"We're still too close to Carson City," Eli said. "When they find those lawmen, there'll be a posse formed up real quick, and they'll be willing to ride a ways in the dark."

"He's right," Rosa said. "We need to keep riding."

Mackie pulled on his reins and got his horse's nose pointed to the west. "Then let's get moving. I know a few places we can hole up."

"Not that way," Rosa interrupted. "We've still got a contract to fulfill."

Not only did Mackie bring his horse back to face her, but he rode up close enough to gaze straight into her eyes. Even in the darkness, he could make out every line in her face when he asked, "Are you crazy? The only thing we need to worry about is staying alive and keeping clear of the hangman's noose. To hell with contracts."

"When we get paid to do a job, we do it. Otherwise, we're no better than some idiot with a gun who hires himself out in a saloon. Folks come to us because they think we can get the tough jobs done."

"Tough jobs, yeah. Sometimes the jobs turn into impossible ones, and there ain't a damn thing we can do about that."

"Are we gonna get moving?" Eli asked. "Because I think I hear someone coming this way."

"Watch yer mouth," Mackie barked. "We're talking here."

"Don't address me that way, mister," Eli said in a steady voice. "I already killed one man for that tonight and I don't mind making it two."

Mackie's eyebrows raised and he started moving toward Eli. "Is that so? Well let's just see about that."

"You two want to fight?" Rosa asked. "Go ahead. You want to die? Just stay here a bit longer and I'm sure some angry lawmen will be glad to help. You want to keep working for me? Stop this petty bullshit and come along."

With that, Rosa snapped her reins and rode in the same general direction Clint had gone a few days ago.

Eli and Mackie swapped a few venomous looks, but they eventually fell into line behind her.

TWENTY-EIGHT

Clint wasn't too worried about catching up to Mr. Galloway. First of all, a man like him was too confident to simply pack up and leave for an unknown period of time after unleashing an assassin onto an innocent man. More than likely, Galloway was sure he'd covered himself from every possible angle and there wasn't anyone smart enough to connect anything to him anyway.

Secondly, there was no reason Galloway would know his plans hadn't been carried out to the letter just yet. Tom Clark wasn't stupid, so he hadn't informed anyone who he had in custody or who'd been killed along the way. That was all the more reason for Galloway to get nice and comfortable while things went to hell outside of his sight.

Third, Clint had needed to rest before climbing back in the saddle and riding all the way back to that Western Union office. The time spent in Carson City had been good. His belly was full and the aches from the last few nicks and bruises he'd collected were fading away. When he actually walked back into that Western Union office, Clint was feeling pretty good.

He felt even better once he saw the surprised expression on Mr. Galloway's face. Galloway was still wearing that expression when he turned around and hurried into his office, leaving a young clerk by himself behind the desk.

The clerk was a man in his late teens wearing glasses. His arms were long and lanky, resembling pieces of wet pasta hanging from his shoulders. Although he seemed puzzled by Galloway's sudden departure, he shrugged it off and faced his customer.

"Hello, sir," the clerk said cheerily. "What can I do for you today?"

"I'd like to see Mr. Galloway," Clint said.

"He's . . . uhh . . . He seems to be busy right now. Is there anything I can do?"

"Yeah. Step aside."

"Pardon me?"

The clerk's first reaction when Clint started walking around the counter was to position himself so that he was blocking Clint's path. Once it was clear that Clint wasn't going to be stopped, the clerk allowed himself to be moved aside without much trouble. Of course, seeing the gun at Clint's side also played a part in that decision.

In a surprisingly quick movement, the clerk hopped over the counter and backed toward the door. The only thing keeping him from bolting was Galloway opening the door to his office on his own.

"I'll get the law, Mr. Galloway," the clerk said in a rush.

Galloway extended his hand and quickly replied, "No need for that! This is probably just some misunderstanding."

"That's right," Clint said without taking his eyes off of Galloway. "A misunderstanding. Mr. Galloway and I are old friends. Isn't that so?"

When Galloway didn't respond right away, the clerk asked, "Is it, Mr. Galloway?"

Before too long, Galloway nodded. "Yes, yes. Of course. I'm just a little surprised to see Mr. Adams. That's all."

"Mind if I have a word with you in private?" Clint asked.

"Not at all." To the clerk, Galloway said, "Watch the office. I'm not to be disturbed."

The clerk tentatively made his way around the counter. After making it to his spot without incident, he said, "All right."

Clint spotted the beads of sweat pushing their way from Galloway's brow. Extending a hand toward the office door, Clint stood so the clerk wouldn't be able to see the older man's tension for himself. "After you."

Galloway walked into his office, and Clint closed the door behind them.

The office was fairly large, but most of that space was taken up by a partner desk which was cluttered by ledgers, papers, and books of all kinds. The right half of the double desk was a bit cleaner, and the chair was pushed neatly in place as if nobody had sat in it recently. Galloway stumbled toward the left side of the desk and leaned on it for support.

"Don't shoot me," Galloway said in a trembling voice. "If you shoot, someone will be here in a heartbeat."

"Why would I want to do that?" Clint asked in a bewildered tone. After letting Galloway sweat for a few seconds, Clint snapped his fingers and said, "That's right! You're probably thinking I might be a little angry after you paid to have me and Johnny Blevin killed."

Clint walked a few steps forward, which put him just inside of arm's reach of Galloway. Lowering his voice to a menacing growl, Clint said, "You'd be right about that."

"It wasn't my idea," Galloway stammered. "It . . . it was his!" he said while jabbing a finger at the empty half of the desk. "He said we could get Blevin's property at a cheap price after he was dead."

"That's a great plan, except you already bought Blevin's property."

Galloway's eyes moved back and forth so quickly in their sockets that they appeared to be rattling around in his head. His lips trembled while tapping on his desk, and the sweat poured over his face as though he'd been standing out in the rain.

"As much as I'd like to hear what you come up with next," Clint said, "I'm too tired to wait around for it. So let me save you some trouble." Grabbing Galloway's shoulder, Clint spun the other man around so he could look him directly in the face. Galloway landed with his back against his desk and yelped as if he'd been nailed there.

"I know it was you who hired those killers," Clint snarled. "Look in my eyes and tell me I'm wrong."

Galloway made a fairly good effort to do just that. Unfortunately, he wasn't able to hold Clint's gaze for more than a few seconds before breaking down. "You're right," he sobbed while hanging his head low. "I wanted to make a deal for less money, but my partner wouldn't have any of it, so I figured I could get that gold back. Blevin was talking so much about traveling when he was paid, and I thought nobody would miss him if he just . . ."

"Disappeared?"

Unable to speak through his trembling, Galloway nodded instead.

"Well, you won't be getting your gold back," Clint told him. "And that assassin you hired is dead."

"Wh-what are you going to do with me?"

"You," Clint said as he dropped a hand onto Galloway's shoulder, "are going to help me get to the bottom of a few things."

TWENTY-NINE

Clint left Galloway's office a while later. The same young clerk was at the desk, and he smiled nervously as Clint tipped his hat to him and walked outside.

Before too much longer, Galloway himself emerged from the office. Dabbing his brow with a wadded handkerchief, he asked, "Has Winston been back yet?"

"No, sir," the clerk replied.

"Well when my illustrious partner does show up again, there is no need to inform him of Mr. Adams's visit."

"Mr. Adams? Was that the man who was just in your—"

"Yes, yes," Galloway snapped. "He was here on business and it doesn't involve anyone but himself and me."

"If Mr. Winston asks, what should I—"

"He won't ask! Just do as I say or you can look for a new job."

"Yes, sir," the clerk replied as if he was about to salute.

Shoving the younger man aside, Galloway said, "Now find something else to do. I have a message that needs to be sent."

"I can do that, sir."

All Galloway had to do was stare at the younger man to get the clerk walking in another direction. Galloway kept right on staring until the clerk turned his back to him and began straightening the papers and pencils on the counter used by customers.

Galloway's hand clutched a pencil and he scribbled quickly on his own paper. After reviewing what he'd written, he shook his head, balled up the paper, and tossed it away. He started again, stopped, and threw that away as well. It wasn't until his fifth attempt that he finally wrote something that wasn't discarded. From there, he stepped over to the telegraph machine and began tapping.

Galloway still sat there until he had his reply. Nodding without writing down what was received, he got up and started to leave the building. He stopped short of the front door, spun around on his heels, marched back to the counter, and dug up the papers he'd discarded from the basket against the wall.

Carrying those balled-up papers in his arm, Galloway walked past the clerk without glancing at the perplexed younger man. He kept right on walking until he was outside and heading for the small saloon directly beside a stagecoach platform.

The bar was about the size of a door and was manned by a smiling fellow in his late forties. There was only enough room in the saloon for four more tables, and Clint sat at the one farthest from the door, against the back wall. As soon as he saw Galloway enter, Clint lifted his beer and smiled.

"It's done," Galloway said as he dropped down into an empty chair across from Clint.

"What is?" Clint asked.

Glancing around, the only other soul Galloway could see was the barkeep. Still smiling, the barkeep nodded and waved.

"You need me to say it?" Galloway asked. "Here?"

"Sorry if I still think you're on the slippery side."

Galloway let out a beleaguered sigh. "I contacted the same people I contacted before about . . . you know."

"Yeah. I know. What did they say?"

"Nothing. It's not like they're sitting back and waiting to hear from me." Leaning forward and dropping his voice to a harsh whisper, Galloway added, "I wasn't even supposed to contact them again."

"Well, I'm certain they're probably aware by now that things didn't exactly go according to plan. What did you say to them?"

"Just that I needed to talk to someone and that it was important. That should be enough to get them to return my message. I'll know the moment their reply comes through."

Clint nodded and sipped his beer. It was good, but not nearly as good as the beer Tom Clark had bought for him in Carson City. "And what do you intend on doing when that reply comes through?"

"Just what you told me to do. I'll ask for someone else to come and finish the job and that they need to be quick about it."

"And?"

Hunkering down so he could press his forehead against his fingertips, Galloway muttered, "And that Mr. Blevin is wrapping up his business here in town."

"Do I need to tell you again not to go anywhere yourself?" Clint asked.

"No."

"Good." With that, Clint got up to leave.

"What do we do now?"

"Wait for the reply."

THIRTY

Over the next two days, Clint checked in on Galloway every couple of hours. He learned from Galloway's partner where to get ahold of the man when he wasn't at the Western Union office, so Clint could even check in on him in the middle of the night.

In actuality, Clint only checked on Galloway a handful of times. He just made sure to do so a twice in a short amount of time and also at odd hours. After that, Galloway was so anxious for the next visit that he felt like he couldn't take one wrong step without being spotted. At least that way, Clint could take care of some business on his own without being too worried about Galloway running off.

One of those points of business to check on was Johnny's house. Clint rode out there to get a look at what remained after the drunks and partygoers finally cleared out. As he expected, there wasn't a whole lot. The fence around the house was knocked down in several places. The little barn was wide open. Even the front door of the house itself swung back and forth on its hinges. As he rode up closer to the house, Clint could make out more than a few windows that were broken now that hadn't been broken before.

Clint couldn't see any movement as he approached the house, but his hand still went reflexively toward the gun at his side.

Leaving Eclipse near the front gate, Clint continued on foot toward Johnny's old front door. Every so often, he could hear something falling and breaking inside the house. A few shuffling steps made their way to Clint's ears, but suddenly stopped.

Clint stopped as well and thought back to what else Galloway could have mentioned in the telegram he'd sent. Since Clint hadn't mentioned a thing regarding where Johnny was truly headed, he wasn't too concerned about putting his friend in danger.

Johnny was most certainly long gone by now. From what Galloway had mentioned, he'd done plenty of talking about traveling and had dropped hints of visiting everywhere from the Amazon to the Far East along the way. All that babbling had paid off in the end by forming something of an ink cloud in Johnny's wake.

Despite the fact that he wasn't worried about Johnny's safety, Clint became more concerned for his own as he tried to get a look at what had happened in Johnny's absence. All he'd truly wanted was to see if those assassins were truly working in some sort of group marked by the fancy weapons they carried. Clint had seen gangs mark themselves by everything from bandannas and sashes to tattoos or pieces of jewelry.

He figured the best, and possibly only, way for him to know if he was dealing with more than one killer was to try and draw a few of them closer. As he walked up to Johnny's place, Clint felt like a hunter approaching a recently sprung trap.

"Hello?" Clint shouted as innocently as he could. "Anyone there?"

For a few moments, the house was quiet as a grave. The few hesitant steps that could be heard made Clint's hand

draw closer to the gun at his side. Suddenly, as if they'd realized there was no more sense in trying to hide, three men
walked out of Johnny's house.

One of them was a kid with short blond hair. He exited
the house with his hands held up and a wide smile on his
face. "Don't shoot. We were just here for the party."

Clint planted his feet and examined all three of the men.
The second to step out of the house was a skinny fellow in
his early twenties. The third had a bulkier frame and wore
battered buckskins decorated with stray bits of fringe
hanging from the sleeves.

"Party's over," Clint said. "It has been for a while."

"Yeah," the blond man said. "We kind of figured that
out for ourselves."

"Then what are you doing there?"

"Do you know where John Blevin is?"

"Why do you ask?"

As if only just spotting the gun in Clint's holster, the
blond man shook his head and started to back into the
house. "Look, mister, we don't want any trouble. Mr.
Blevin threw a party and said we could stay as long as we
wanted. He left and we haven't heard from him since. I was
hoping to stay on for another day or two until we
scrounged up our horses."

The man in the buckskins nodded once and added,
"Some asshole stole our animals. If you know about that,
I'd like the chance to wring the bastard's neck."

"I'll bet you would," Clint said. "Are there any more of
you in there?"

"No, sir," the blond replied. "Everyone else wandered
off, but not before doing their share of damage. Bunch of
animals if you ask me."

"And you three didn't have anything to do with that, I
suppose?"

Before responding to Clint's question, the three men
glanced back and forth at one another as if they were each

afraid to speak first. Finally, the blond looked back to Clint and said, "I guess we did, but it was one hell of a party. Were you there for any of it yourself?"

"Yeah," Clint said as he thought back to the chaos that had greeted him when he'd first arrived. "I was there for a bit."

"You didn't see anyone stealing horses, did you?"

"Actually, someone tried to help themselves to that animal right over there," Clint said as he hooked a thumb back toward Eclipse.

"You're lucky you spotted the prick in time," the man in the buckskins said. "I hope you put a good hurtin' on him."

Clint nodded. "He didn't get what he was after, that's for certain."

All three of them men had allowed their shoulders to relax by now. Two of them even approached Clint. The skinny one only took a few steps from the front door of the house before coming to a stop.

"Think you could tell us where Mr. Blevin went?" the blond asked. "We'd sure like to thank him for his hospitality."

Clint wasn't about to say anything of the sort to anyone who'd simply squatted on Johnny's property after drinking all his beer. His guard came up even more when he spotted the glint of a sapphire stickpin on the skinny man's collar.

THIRTY-ONE

At first, the glint of light off the sapphire seemed to come from a button. After seeing the first hint of blue in that sparkle, Clint knew exactly what he was looking at. More importantly, he realized who he was looking at.

"Actually, Johnny isn't too far from here," Clint said.

Hearing that brought another sort of glint into the eyes of all three of the other men.

"Really?" the one in buckskins asked. "We'd sure appreciate an introduction."

"Or better yet," the blond one said, "you could just point us in the right direction."

"Sure thing," Clint said as he turned and walked toward the gate. Even though his stride was casual enough, his ears were sharply attuned for any sound that could be threatening. All he heard was two of the men coming up behind him.

Stopping in his tracks, Clint said, "But first, wouldn't you like to know what happened to that Spanish friend of yours?"

None of the other three said anything right away.

Then, the blond one asked, "Spanish friend?"

"You know the one I mean. His name was . . . oh yeah! Dominguez."

As he said that name, Clint pivoted on the balls of his feet until he'd turned completely around and squared off against all three men. His expression was still leaning to the friendly side and his hand wasn't too close to his Colt, but his eyes didn't stray from the other three men for one second.

The man in the buckskins leaned forward a bit until he resembled an animal getting ready to pounce.

The skinny fellow stayed where he was. His hand was now setting on top of the grip of his own holstered pistol.

The blond maintained his smile, but something in his eyes told Clint that he knew he'd been found out. "That name don't sound familiar."

"It doesn't? Then I suppose you don't care if he was killed a few days ago." Clint didn't see any of the men react too much to that, but he could sense that all three were starting to squirm. "He had a thing for sapphires, too. Just like you boys and those pretty pins you're wearing."

With that, the smile on the blond's face disappeared. The other two took on more serious expressions as well, as their muscles tensed.

Being the closest one to Clint, the blond man acted first. He started to take a step back, but made a quick reach for his gun instead. As he drew the pistol from its holster, he dropped to one knee.

Clint waited just long enough to see how the others would react. The moment he realized that the remaining two were following the blond's lead, Clint plucked the modified Colt from his holster and aimed from the hip. He pulled his trigger and watched as his bullet followed along his own line of sight to tear a bloody hole through the blond's chest.

The blond still got a shot off, but it was more of a reflex

than anything else. His finger clamped tightly around the trigger as his body reacted to being shot. As he fell back onto his bent leg, the blond's other leg splayed out in front of him as his shoulders hit the dirt.

Standing only a few paces behind the blond, the man in buckskins jumped to one side as soon as he saw Clint clear leather. He drew and fired a shot to cover himself, but scrambled behind a nearby water trough without looking to see what he'd hit.

When Clint shifted his eyes to the house, he was just able to catch a glimpse of the skinny man's foot as he ducked in through the front door. There wasn't any cover nearby, so Clint hunkered down a bit and circled to his left while watching for one of the other two to make a move.

The first thing to catch Clint's attention was the shattering of glass. One of the windows next to the door was broken from the inside as the skinny man used the butt of a rifle to clear it out. Rather than take a shot, however, he paused to stare at Clint over the top of his barrel.

Like another part of the same machine, the man in buckskins took full advantage of the skinny man's distraction and fired his own gun while Clint was looking at the house.

Clint was starting to fire a shot in response to the one the skinny man had taken at him, but he ducked and turned when he caught a glimpse of the man in buckskins rising up from behind the trough. Clint's finger tightened around his trigger as his body dropped. Once on the ground, Clint rolled toward the house and kept firing at the trough.

Chunks of wood flew in every direction as the trough was hit again and again by incoming rounds. The man in buckskins fired from behind it but only hit the ground. He kept shooting, even as he saw Clint roll beneath the rickety front porch.

Once under the crooked boards, Clint flipped open the cylinder of his Colt and emptied out the spent rounds. He didn't have much room to maneuver, so he wasn't able to look at what he was doing as he reloaded. That didn't pose much of a problem, since Clint could have taken fresh bullets from his gun belt and slid them into place with his eyes shut.

The skinny man leaned out the window, but quickly pulled himself back in as more bullets tore through the house from behind the trough. "Hold yer goddamn fire!" he shouted.

Nodding quickly, the man in buckskins stood up and began reloading his own weapon. In between fitting in the fresh rounds, he jabbed a finger toward the bottom of the house. From the window, the skinny man nodded.

Gripping his shotgun in both hands, the skinny man aimed at the floor and squinted through the dust and smoke that now swirled through the air. He flinched at every bit of movement he saw, right down to the insects that skittered across the floorboards. Finally, the skinny man held his breath and stayed perfectly still so he could listen.

For a few seconds, he only heard wind whistling through the broken windows.

Then, the sounds of his partner moving outside reached his ears.

Eventually, the skinny man picked up the crunch of something dragging over the packed dirt beneath the house itself.

The skinny man slowly moved forward. He barely made a sound as he placed one foot carefully in front of the other. All the while, he kept his eyes glued to the floor and his ears open for another sign pointing to where Clint might have gone.

There was another muffled crunch, which stopped just as quickly as it had started. As the skinny man leaned down a bit more, he stared through a dark space between two loose boards. He thought he might have seen something move under the boards and took aim just to be certain.

Suddenly, he realized something was under the floor. He could see the glint of light reflecting off of something smooth and rounded. By the time he realized he was looking at the barrel of a gun, it was too late.

Clint pulled his trigger and sent a pair of bullets up through the floor. His first shot sparked against the skinny man's shotgun and knocked the weapon aside as thunder exploded from its twin barrels. The sound of the second shot was lost amid the noise of the others, but managed to widen the hole in the floor.

Now looking up from the opening he'd made, Clint kept pulling his trigger until his bullets drew blood. The skinny man reeled backward and dropped his shotgun. When his body hit the floor, it covered Clint with a thick layer of dust that had been loosed from the floor. Just to be certain, Clint adjusted his aim and fired at the dark shape above him.

The skinny man twitched as the bullets tore through him, but he didn't move much more than that. At that point, the only thing left for him to do was bleed.

Clint went through the motions of reloading once more as he pushed himself against the ground using both legs. By the time his snapped the Colt shut, his head was emerging from beneath the house and he rolled onto his belly so he could scramble into the fresh air.

A shot was fired from the front door.

Clint stayed low and waited a second before stretching up to look through one of the broken windows at the rear of the house. All he could see from that angle was the shadow of the man in buckskins moving into the front room.

Seeing the body of his partner laying on the broken floor was enough for the remaining man to piece together what had happened. While firing a shot into the floor, the man in buckskins jumped outside and prepared to fire at the first thing he saw moving beneath the house.

Although he did spot some movement, it wasn't from beneath the house.

Bringing his gun around, the man in buckskins turned toward the house's right corner.

Clint rounded the corner, straightened his arm, and fired his Colt. That bullet whipped through the air and drilled a messy hole through the other man's head.

After making sure there weren't any more assassins lurking about, Clint jumped onto Eclipse's back and rode to town.

THIRTY-TWO

The Western Union office was full of people as Clint brought Eclipse to a stop in front of it. Since it was nearing the end of business hours, several people formed a line at the front desk, milled around within the office, and stood at the various tables inside.

Clint swung down from his saddle and strode through the front door, ignoring the annoyed comments he got from the folks that needed to be pushed aside. Glancing from one face to another, Clint didn't find anyone who looked familiar. He also didn't spot a single sapphire.

"We're busy right now," the young clerk behind the desk announced. "You'll have to wait your turn like everyone else."

"Where's Galloway?" Clint asked.

The clerk was about the same age as the one that had been there on Clint's previous visits, but he wasn't the same man. This one wore a dented visor over an angular face and had a very pronounced overbite. Even though he looked light enough to be pushed over by a stiff breeze, he didn't even flinch when Clint stormed toward the counter.

"Mr. Galloway's in his office," the clerk said. "But you'll have to wait if you want to see him."

Before all of the clerk's words could get out of his mouth, Clint was shoving through more people so he could get to the door at the back of the room marked PRIVATE.

"Sir, you're not allowed in there!" the clerk shouted. As he started to move around the counter, his arm was grabbed by the customer at the front of the line.

"That message needs to be sent!" the customer snapped. "And you'll send it right now or I'll have my money back!"

"Yes, sir." To Clint, the clerk said, "I'm having you thrown out of here!" The clerk looked around frantically, but couldn't find the person he was searching for.

The only other clerk in the place had already met Clint and had made himself scarce rather than lift a finger against him.

Although Clint wasn't too concerned about either of the clerks, he was relieved to hear the customers assert themselves enough to hold the young man's attention. Galloway's office was unlocked, so Clint stepped inside and immediately shut the door behind him.

Galloway was in there, all right. Unfortunately, he wasn't in any condition to talk.

"God damn it," Clint muttered as he spotted the man laying facedown on his half of the double-sided desk.

Galloway's arms were positioned in a way that made him look like a doll that had been tossed over a child's shoulder. One rested on a pile of papers, and the other dangled from his shoulder and knocked against one set of drawers.

His eyes were as wide open as his mouth.

As a matter of fact, Galloway's eyes were also open as wide as his throat.

Clint moved toward the desk and his hand rested on the grip of his pistol. The scent of blood hung in the air like a thick, rusty fog. It filled his nose and crept far enough down his throat to trigger a few reflexive gags. After moving one of Galloway's arms aside, Clint was able to see the gash that stretched ear-to-ear along Galloway's neck.

Having seen more than his share of knife wounds, Clint could tell this one had been made by one hell of a sharp blade. The edges of the wound were smooth and neat. The wound was so big that it also made it difficult for him to guess how long Galloway had been laying there. When he heard someone opening the door behind him, Clint turned on his heels and nearly drew his Colt.

"Mr. Galloway, I can . . . Good Lord!" the clerk sputtered as he recoiled at the sight of Galloway's body. "You . . . killed him?"

"He was like this when I found him," Clint replied. "Who came into this office last?"

The clerk looked as if he was about to say something, but then started backing out the door. Just as he whipped around to bolt out of the office, he was stopped by a vise-like grip around his wrist.

Rather than draw his gun, Clint used that same speed to grab hold of the clerk and stop him from running away. With another quick motion, he pulled the clerk in as if he were reeling in a fish. "Who was the last one in here?" Clint snarled.

"Don't kill me! I swear, I'll keep quiet, just don't kill me!"

"I didn't kill anyone. Open your eyes and maybe you could see as much for yourself."

The clerk opened his eyes a bit, but it seemed to take more effort than if he'd used a lever.

"I've been in this room for less than a minute," Clint said. "Less than half a minute, actually. There's no way for a man to get his throat cut, fall over, and bleed out that much in that amount of time."

Although he didn't say anything, the clerk took another look at Galloway's body. He was also struggling a bit less against Clint's grip.

"Now look at me," Clint said quickly. "Do you see any blood on me?"

"No."

"Do you really think I did this and then stuck around here now rather than put you down as well on my way out?"

Losing some of the color in his face, the clerk shook his head again. "I guess not."

"Good," Clint said as he slowly released the clerk's arm. "Now tell me who else was in here besides Galloway."

"There was someone."

"How long ago?"

"Half an hour or so. It's kind of hard to tell since it got so busy after that."

"Do you know who it was?" Clint asked.

Slowly, the clerk shook his head. "No, but there was some noise in here after she arrived, and when she walked out, she was pulling on a coat. I just thought they were . . . you know."

"Yeah," Clint sighed. "I'm pretty sure I do know."

THIRTY-THREE

The hotel wasn't close to the Western Union office, but it wasn't so far that it couldn't be reached easily by foot. Rosa covered the distance even quicker than normal because she was practically skipping all the way back to her room.

She waved to the man at the front desk and went up the stairs to the room she'd rented not too long ago. After a few quick knocks, the door came open and she could see a sliver of a face peeking out at her. Rosa stared right back at that one eye and pushed the door open.

"Damn, woman," Mackie growled as he stepped back and pressed a hand to his chin. "You almost knocked my head off."

Rosa drifted past him and let her fingertips brush against his face. "Awww," she purred. "You want Momma to kiss it and make it better?"

"That'd be nice."

"The way I feel right now, I might actually make good on that." As she said those words, Rosa peeled the coat off her shoulders and let it fall to the floor. She wore a light brown dress that had a bit of lace on the collar. Dark stains were spattered across her skirt, most of which resembled dark red paint that had flown off a brush in a single, sweeping stroke.

The longer Mackie and Eli looked at her, the more dark red spots they saw. Some were on the bottom of her skirt, and several smaller ones were on her blouse. A few of the drops had even made it to the base of her neck. Rosa licked her fingers and slowly wiped those away.

"It's done," she said.

Mackie took another look at the hallway before closing and locking the door. "I can see that much. Where'd you find him?"

"In his office. All I had to do was convince his partner to leave us alone."

"Blevin had an office?"

"He wasn't there."

Furrowing his brow, Mackie asked, "Then who the hell are you talking about?"

"Galloway."

"Galloway, as in the man who hired you?"

"Hired us," she corrected.

Eli had been sitting with his back to a wall cleaning his gun. His legs were resting on the edge of the bed, and the parts of his pistol were situated on a cloth spread over his lap. "Why would you do that?" he asked.

Arching her back as if she were modeling the latest fashion from Paris, Rosa glanced over to Eli and said, "Shut your mouth. You don't get to question me yet."

"All right," Mackie said as he stepped between the other two. "I've been with you for a while, so I hope that counts for something."

"Sure it does," Rosa said as she ran her hands over the front of her bloody dress.

"Then tell me, why would you do that?"

Eli shook his head and chuckled under his breath as he finished his cleaning and began fitting his gun back together.

"I went to see him just like we discussed," she replied.

"I asked him what happened and where Blevin got off to. He couldn't tell me a damn thing."

"And you don't think he might have known something useful if you would've taken the time to ask nicely? Jesus Christ, Rosa, bending men around your little finger is yer goddamn specialty."

She smiled. "I started, but he wouldn't have any of it. He just talked about all the trouble that's been going on since he hired us. He also mentioned how he might just have to forget about this whole thing and hire someone else. He even mentioned going to the law."

"That's bullshit and you know it," Mackie grunted. "He's in too deep to go to the law."

"Yes, but he still wanted this job done, and he sure as hell would go to someone else to get it done." Spinning so she was facing Mackie straight on, Rosa added, "And are you willing to bet that he wouldn't mention who had this job before?

"Even if he let one of our names slip, odds are someone might know who he's talking about. We can't afford to be connected to a mess like this. We're known as people who can be trusted on any job. When someone hires a Sapphire, someone winds up dead. That's how it is and that's how it'll stay."

"I don't think that someone should be our client," Mackie said. "That might not do wonders for our reputation either, you know."

Rosa reached out to slide her fingertips along the bottom of Mackie's chin. "I know, but that client won't be telling anything to anyone. Nobody even needs to know he was a client."

When he saw Rosa turn to throw a warning glance at him, Eli held up his hands and said, "Ain't nobody hearing anything from me."

That seemed to be good enough for her, so she nodded and turned her attention back to Mackie. Rosa put an exaggerated pout on her face and placed both hands on his face. Leaning forward so her lips were brushing against his ear, she asked, "Are you mad at me?"

"I'm just not sure this was the best thing to do," he said. "I mean, we should be laying low after the way we left Carson City."

"Nobody even lifted a finger to stop me from doing whatever I wanted in that place," Rosa said with a smile. "And now we can keep our heads held high and our winning streak going. If anyone asks, we've never even heard of Galloway or Blevin."

"All right, then. Before you get too busy patting yerself on the back, you should know them other three youngbloods we called out here ain't never showed up again."

"You mean the ones who were supposed to check out the Blevin place?"

"Them are the ones," Mackie said.

"I might know what happened to them," Rosa told him. "Mr. Galloway brought up a name just before he died."

"Was it the name of someone good enough to take down three armed men all by himself?"

Rosa smiled and nodded. "All that and more. He's even good enough to put one hell of a feather in the Sapphires' caps once word gets around that it was us who killed him."

THIRTY-FOUR

Clint waved to the man behind the front desk of his hotel on his way to the little dining room. It wasn't too late to get something for supper, but he wasn't going to expect anything to be too fresh, either. Just as he caught the scent of baked chicken, Clint heard the man behind the desk shout his name.

"Mr. Adams! Someone was asking for you."

"Was it the sheriff?" Clint asked. "Because I've already had a word with him."

"No, not the sheriff. She said you both were friends of John Blevin."

Hearing that put Clint on his toes. His hand drifted toward his pistol as he took a quick look around. As near as he could tell, the only people in sight either worked at the hotel or were eating there. "It's a she?" he asked.

"Most definitely."

"Did you get her name?"

The clerk winced and shook his head. "Not as such. She was in a hurry."

"What did she want?"

"I don't know, but I told her you might be back for dinner."

Clint nodded and started walking into the dining room. "That's where I'm headed now. If she comes back, point her my way."

"Will do."

After spotting a table against the wall, Clint walked across the small room and wove between the few other occupied tables. Since he was expecting to see some pretty woman wearing a sapphire pin coming straight at him, the walk seemed doubly long. Clint made it to his seat without incident, though, and put his back to the wall so he could watch the rest of the room.

His eyes were so intense that the girl who walked over to take his order lost her smile by the time she opened her mouth.

"What can I get for you, sir?" she asked quickly and without returning his stare.

Clint realized how nervous he was making the poor girl and softened his features with a smile. "Sorry about that. I was drifting off. What's good here?"

The effect was immediate and caused the girl to let out a breath and put on a smile of her own. "We've still got some chicken pot pies left."

"I'll have one and some water."

"Coming right up." Even though she was much more at ease, she was still anxious to get away from Clint's table and back into the kitchen.

The water was brought to his table, and the food came shortly after that. Clint dug into the pot pie and quickly found himself tearing through the tender meat and flaky crust. When he looked up to find a woman staring intently at him from across the room, Clint met her gaze and wiped his mouth with the corner of his napkin.

She moved toward him slowly at first. Then, once she was two tables away, she hurried to one of the empty chairs at Clint's table and sat down.

"I'm so glad you're back," she said.

Clint was still a bit surprised when he nodded at her. One hand held his napkin on top of the table, and the other was resting on the grip of his holstered Colt. "I . . . wasn't expecting you, Victoria."

The blond woman wore a dark blue skirt and a simple brown top that was buttoned all the way up to her neck. Compared to the woman that had spent a good amount of Johnny's party rolling in the hay with Clint, she almost looked like a completely different person.

"Did the man tell you I was looking for you earlier?" she asked.

Clint reflexively looked toward the lobby and nodded. "He mentioned someone was asking about me, but he didn't say who it was."

Victoria was flustered and out of breath. Her eyes nervously darted to and fro, making her seem even more guarded than Clint had been. "That was me, all right. I know you and Johnny were friends, and after I heard about what happened to him, I hoped you might have come back to check on him for yourself."

"What happened to Johnny?" Clint asked.

"He's gone! He's just gone. His house is cleaned out. His horses are gone. His wagon's gone. Everything's just . . . gone."

Clint relaxed a bit. "Were you and him close?"

"We were friends, but not as close as you and I were," she replied with a guilty little grin. "He talked about you a bit and hoped you would show up at the party. After that, I haven't heard much of anything from him."

"Well, he didn't make a big announcement but he's moved on."

"Really? To where?"

"Last I heard, he was heading west," Clint said. Since he figured Johnny would have told her if he'd wanted her to know, he left it at that. Fortunately, that seemed to be enough for Victoria.

She let out another breath and smiled. "As long as he's all right. Mind if I join you for dinner?"

"Not at all."

THIRTY-FIVE

Victoria had half a pot pie, and Clint kept her company as his own food settled. He suggested dessert, but then she made a better suggestion that involved going up to his room. A few minutes later, they were out of their clothes and under the sheets.

Clint's room was a small space occupied by a narrow bed, a table, and two chairs. The only light in the room at the moment came from a lantern holding a flame that was just big enough to be seen. Clint pumped his hips between Victoria's open legs with growing intensity, until the head-board knocked against the wall.

Beneath him, Victoria closed her eyes and arched her back while letting out a slow, panting moan. Suddenly, her breath caught in her throat and her fingers clenched tightly around Clint's hands. Her orgasm swept through her and nearly stole her last bit of breath away before Clint thrust once more into her.

Clint remained inside of her until his climax faded. Only then did he roll to one side and scoop her up with one arm to hold against him. She lay with her cheek resting on his chest and her leg draped across his hips.

"That sure beat the hell out of that barn," she said breathlessly.

"Yes, indeed."

"I've been thinking plenty about that barn, you know. Every time I did, I hoped to get another go at you."

Clint chuckled and rubbed her shoulder. "I hope I didn't disappoint you."

"Are you kidding? I still haven't caught my breath."

"I'm surprised you found me. After all, it's not like anyone knew I was coming."

"I didn't know either," she said. "I was just checking the hotel registers looking to see if Johnny was here. I saw your name and thought you might know where he went."

Even in the darkness, Clint had been careful to keep his face unreadable. That point he'd just raised had bothered him since he saw Victoria in the dining room, and those few words put his mind at ease. "So how well did you know Johnny?" he asked, addressing another thing that had been under his skin.

"He's lived here for a while," she said simply. "I would see him most of the times when he came into town. I was a little worried about folks trying to take advantage of his hospitality when he told everyone about that party of his, and I guess I got even more worried when he went missing afterward. You must think I'm awfully suspicious."

"Not at all, especially when compared to some other people I know."

"Maybe just a busybody, then."

"Yeah," Clint said as he stretched out. "That sounds more like it."

Victoria responded with a playful jab to his ribs. "I heard Johnny came into some money. Is that true?"

"He must have come into enough money to pay for that party he threw."

"Could be. I think a lot of that food was brought by

neighbors and such. Everybody liked Johnny even though he didn't talk much."

"There you go, then. I know he headed west, and that's about it."

"So what brings you back here?" Victoria asked.

"I wanted to check and see if he left anything important behind. There were some horse thieves at that party, and I didn't want them doing any more damage than they already did. Other than that, I was just stopping here for a rest until I moved on myself."

"Did you hear about those two men from Western Union?"

Clint felt his stomach clench and his muscles tighten even worse than they had been before. "I know Mr. Galloway was found dead. Was there another?"

He could feel Victoria's head brushing against his chest as she nodded. "The other man who ran that office. I think it was Mr. Galloway's partner."

"What happened to him?"

"He was killed in his home. I hear he was found in his own bed, naked as a jaybird."

"Who would want to do a thing like that?" Clint asked, trying not to sound as anxious as he felt.

"I don't know, but he was a mess when they found him. At least, that's what I heard."

Sitting up and turning to look at Victoria's face, Clint asked, "How did you come across all this information?"

The tone in his voice alone was enough to send a chill under Victoria's skin. "I just . . . heard it. This isn't a very big town, you know. People talk, especially when something like this happens. What's the matter, Clint? Why are you looking at me like that?"

Although the lantern was only throwing off a weak excuse for light, it was enough for Clint to see the fear on Victoria's face. The longer he looked at her, the more she recoiled, until she was about to slide off the side of the bed.

"What's wrong, Clint? You're scaring me."

"Nothing's wrong. That's just some troubling news. Two men killed in one day."

"I don't know if it was in one day, but they were both only found recently. Did you know them?"

"I've done some business with Galloway, but I only met his partner once."

"What kind of business?"

"Nothing much, really," Clint lied. "But I was one of the first to see him after he was killed."

"Oh God," Victoria said as she straightened up and put her hand to her mouth. "That's terrible. No wonder you're so nervous."

"Yeah," Clint said as he walked over to the corner where all their clothes had wound up. "I should probably see if there's anything I can do to help with all of this." As he picked up his own clothes, Clint sifted through Victoria's as well.

He felt the dress and blouse she'd been wearing and found nothing more than buttons and cloth. Her boots were old and weren't holding anything but a worn set of laces. Her underthings were so thin and frilly that they didn't need to be inspected. When he was done, Clint felt a little embarrassed to be poking through her things like that.

"I need to go," he said while pulling on his clothes. "If you want to stay here, you're more than welcome."

Victoria got up and walked over to him. She stood next to the pile of her clothes without making another move toward them. Instead, she wrapped her arms around Clint and leaned forward to kiss him on the lips. "I live here in town, remember?" she asked gently. "I can get home just fine."

"All right."

Clint walked to the chair between the bed and the window where he'd left his holster. While buckling the Colt around his waist, he heard the sounds of Victoria's movements come to a stop. When he turned around, he found her standing there with her clothes on, but not fully buttoned.

With a solemn look on her face she asked him, "Did I do something wrong?"

"No. It's just odd to have men turn up dead not long after I've talked to them. I guess it just doesn't set right."

"If something else happens, do you think I could stay here with you?"

"It doesn't set right with you, either, huh?"

She shook her head.

"If you think I'd have any objection to you staying here, you must not have been paying attention for the last hour or so."

Victoria laughed and finished dressing. "I thought you might say something like that."

THIRTY-SIX

"What the hell do you mean there's no investigation?" Clint asked.

The man in front of him was a stout fellow in his late forties. Although his face was clean-shaven, he had the look about him of a man who'd have a hard time growing a beard if he wanted to. His only response to Clint's sudden display of temper was to raise his hands as well as his voice so he could be heard clearly.

"It's not that there's going to be no investigation, Mr. Adams," the stout man said. "It's just that I won't be conducting it."

Clint took half a step back and looked the man up and down. Sure enough, there was a badge pinned to the man's chest and a gun belt around his waist. "You're the law around here, aren't you?" Clint asked, just to be sure.

"Yes, I am."

"And you do know two men were killed today?"

"Yes, I do," the man replied with a bit more annoyance in his voice.

Clint looked him up and down once more and then shook his head. "Then maybe you could help me out here.

I don't see why you'd be dragging your feet unless you had some reason to let a murderer go free."

The lawman reared up and cocked his head to one side. "Now, see here! Nobody's letting a murderer go free, and I resent what you're implying."

"Really? Then I suppose you figure those men died of natural causes?"

"Of course not. I just don't have to explain my actions to you, sir!"

Even though he wasn't too concerned about overstepping his bounds, Clint could tell he wasn't going to get anywhere if the lawman's guard was raised and fortified. He nodded and eased up just enough to make the stout man think he'd had something to do with backing Clint down.

"You may know that Mr. Blevin and I conducted some recent business with Mr. Galloway," Clint said.

The lawman's voice matched Clint's more relaxed tone. "I am aware of that."

"Then you can understand why I'm a little upset."

"Actually, I do."

"Then could you tell me what's going to be done about these murders?"

Finally, the lawman let out a deep breath and hooked his thumbs through his belt as if he was getting ready to cut loose with a grand announcement. "Certainly," he said. "There will be a Pinkerton agent arriving within the next day or two."

Clint stood quietly waiting for the rest of the announcement. When it was clear that the lawman was through, Clint asked, "That's it?"

"Are you familiar with the Pinkerton Agency? They're quite capable."

"I know who the Pinkertons are. What will you be doing until they arrive?"

The lawman furrowed his brow and looked around as if

he thought someone might be playing a trick on him. "What else needs to be done?"

"So you just contact the Pinkertons and then wait for them to get here?"

"I didn't call them. Western Union did."

"That's interesting," Clint said.

"If you want to ask any more questions, I recommend you address them to Western Union. Now, if you don't mind, I have work to do."

Clint laughed to himself and turned his back to the lawman. "Sure. I'll just bet you're busy with all the bigger problems around here."

The lawman sputtered something in his defense, but Clint didn't stay around long enough to hear it. In fact, it was all he could do to keep himself from taking a swing at the stout man just to knock the dumb look off his face.

Clint stomped out of the lawman's office and jumped onto Eclipse's back so he could race to the Western Union office. Even though the dark wouldn't have been much of a hindrance, since the area was mostly flat and the Western Union office was easy enough to see, he knew he'd only be madder if he took the time to walk rather than ride.

He arrived at the Western Union office amid a thunder of hooves and dropped down from the saddle before Eclipse even came to a full stop. From there, Clint walked to the door and pulled the knob. It was locked.

Looking through all the windows he could find, Clint couldn't see the first hint of movement inside the place. In fact, considering the conversation he'd just had, he wouldn't have been surprised if Galloway was still stinking up his office.

THIRTY-SEVEN

Clint woke up early the next morning, had breakfast downstairs, and took some extra time to savor another cup of coffee. He found a copy of the local newspaper folded up on the front desk, but saw that it was almost a week old. He read it anyway while sitting on a rocking chair situated on the boardwalk just outside the hotel.

The streets weren't busy, but they weren't empty, either. Most of the horses were showing up a little farther away, where the Western Union office and stagecoach platforms had been built. Clint counted half a dozen coaches coming and going as he sat and read the newspaper. Some of the new arrivals made their way into town, but most of them stayed just long enough to catch another coach and be on their way.

At first, Clint was aggravated that nobody seemed too concerned with finding out what had happened to the Western Union men. Then, he decided to let the law do whatever they wanted. The town was small enough that all Clint needed to do to keep abreast of any major happenings was keep his eyes and ears open.

If another body was found, he would hear about it.

If someone was killing those left in Johnny's wake, they would soon be after Clint.

And if someone was after Clint, sooner or later they would find him.

By sitting out in plain sight and keeping a lookout, Clint figured he would be found sooner rather than later.

In fact, he had to wait even less than he figured.

Clint was about done with his paper. He leaned back in his chair with his legs crossed and the paper held up in front of him. Although he was able to read easily enough, he was also able to watch the street over the top of the paper. There were only a few buildings in front of him, which meant relatively few windows to watch.

Spotting the man across the street, Clint glanced at him over the top of the newspaper to get a better look. Sure enough, the man was looking at him. He was also armed. Clint lowered the paper, folded it, and set it down beside his chair. He then got up and locked eyes with the other man.

Mackie stared back at him. His hand remained close to his own holster, but not so close as to raise an eyebrow.

Holding his ground, Clint took another look around. It wasn't so easy now, since he had to make certain not to let Mackie out of his sight. He managed to keep the other man in his field of vision as he searched for anyone else positioned in a way that might mark them as Mackie's backup. As far as Clint could tell, Mackie was the only one he needed to be concerned about. When Clint took one step toward the street, Mackie turned his back on him and walked around to the back of a shop facing the hotel.

Clint let the other man go, knowing all too well that the one spot he couldn't check was the top of the hotel itself. As much as he wanted to have a word with that other man, he wasn't about to walk into the open and put his back to a possible marksman along the way.

Instead, Clint hurried into the hotel and bolted up the

stairs. He nearly stampeded over a short Chinese woman carrying an armful of blankets down the hall.

"How do I get to the roof?" Clint asked.

"Why the roof?"

Rather than coming up with a likely story, Clint produced a silver dollar from his pocket and slipped it between her hand and the bottommost blanket.

"A ladder goes to the attic," she said. "It's in the closet there."

Clint looked to where she nodded and saw the narrow, unmarked door just outside of his reach. Leaning that way, he opened the door and saw the brooms and buckets piled on the floor. There was also a short length of rope dangling from a hatch in the ceiling.

"Much obliged," Clint said with a tip of his hat.

The Chinese woman muttered something about the sanity of white men as she continued about her business.

Clint could already hear footsteps pounding over his head as he tugged on the rope and brought the rickety ladder down. One of the old rungs started to snap as he climbed the ladder, but Clint was moving too fast to break it all the way through.

The attic was a dirty space that felt like a cross between a coffin and a stove. Angular walls closed in on him, forcing Clint to hunker down as he shuffled across the floor. By the time he found the hatch leading to the roof, the hot, dusty air had almost completely run out. Clint gasped for breath as he pushed open the door and stuck his head outside.

Although the roof was slightly angled, it was a whole lot easier for Clint to keep his balance up there than it had been to move through the attic. To his right was the back of the hotel's main sign. To his left was a good portion of the roof itself. Directly in front of him was one of the steeper slopes as well as a slender figure running toward the edge with a rifle in his hand.

As Clint sped to try and catch up to the other man, his

boot skidded on a few loose shingles. His other leg stomped forward to catch his weight as his left arm swung out to try and grab hold of something to keep from falling. Clint managed to regain his balance before dropping off the side, and he immediately broke into a run.

After a few close calls, Clint got the hang of moving on the roof. Unfortunately, the man he'd spotted had already jumped onto the roof of the neighboring building.

Common sense screamed at Clint to take a moment and look before he leapt.

The rest of his body and mind overruled that sound advice, and his legs pumped even harder to gain more steam before reaching the edge of the roof. He got there all too soon, and Clint planted one foot on the edge while stretching out with his other leg.

It wasn't until he was hanging there, three floors up with nothing but air between himself and the ground, that Clint realized he might have just made a big mistake.

THIRTY-EIGHT

The tip of Clint's boot scraped against the edge of the neighboring roof. In the split second that followed, he swore the next thing he would feel was the snapping of his bones as he dropped to the ground. What he actually felt was the bottom of his other boot knocking against the roof and skidding along its surface.

Rather than take any time to count his blessings, Clint used the rest of his momentum to lunge forward before his first leg slipped all the way off the side. That foot didn't find a grip anywhere, but only knocked against the edge before he was able to pull himself up. Gritting his teeth against the biting pain in his shin, Clint looked for the man he was after.

While Clint had almost made a mistake in jumping between rooftops, the other man made a mistake by watching him do it. Now that Clint obviously wasn't going to fall, the other man turned his back to him and kept moving.

The next building over was a bit shorter and wider, which made it an easier jump. The man Clint was chasing cleared the gap with ease and was running as soon as his boots hit the roof.

As he charged toward the far edge of the hotel's roof,

Clint watched where the other man was headed and figured he could make up some ground by running along the front side of that building. Adding a bit more steam into his steps, Clint took off much better than he had before and sailed through the air to land hard on both feet.

The jolt of the landing sent a ripple through his legs and a few sparks of pain through his knees, but Clint got moving again without too much effort. As he'd figured, the other man was running at an angle toward him and should meet up with Clint before either man reached the next jump.

Clint was close enough to see a bit more of the man he was after. He couldn't make out much of his face, but Clint could see the dark color of the man's skin and the guns he wore. Since Eli had yet to look over his shoulder at him, Clint fixed his eyes upon the black man's back like a hawk swooping in for the kill.

Suddenly, a shot cracked from the street and blew a chunk of wood a few inches from Clint's feet. Clint's first reaction was to turn and look while also heading for cover. That awkward combination of movements was almost enough to trip him up for good, but Clint kept himself upright. Slowing himself down, he looked over the edge of the roof to find Mackie standing on the boardwalk across the street from the hotel.

Clint got a fleeting glimpse of Mackie sighting down his barrel, which caused him to dive for the roof. Before his hands even slapped against the hot shingles on top of the hotel, Clint heard the second shot fired from Mackie's gun.

Lead whipped over Clint's head. All he had to do from there was roll away from the front of the roof and he was no longer able to be seen from street level. That only left him with one more person to deal with, and he wasn't about to let Eli get away so easily.

Keeping his head low, Clint got his legs beneath him and started running again. He could see Eli heading for the edge of the roof and looking back before jumping. Clint drew his modified Colt and aimed as if he were simply pointing his finger.

Clint waited for Eli to reach the edge of the roof.

He waited a bit more, until Eli built up his speed.

The moment Eli pushed off from the edge of the roof, Clint fired a shot which caught Eli as if he were a can that had been tossed into the air for target practice.

Eli let out a pained yelp and dropped.

Clint couldn't tell how well Eli had landed, but he knew the black man wouldn't be running so quickly anymore. Before Eli got a chance to collect himself and move on, Clint rushed toward the front of the building and ducked behind a rectangular sign. When he peeked over the top of it, Clint saw Mackie crossing the street while looking toward the spot where Eli had made his jump.

Clint looked down and realized he was much closer to the ground than he had been on top of the hotel. Since it seemed as though Mackie hadn't caught sight of him just yet, Clint moved behind the sign as Mackie walked below him.

After all that shooting, Mackie was the only one left on the street. Clint apologized under his breath for anyone he might have missed as he slammed his shoulder against one corner of the sign and fired a shot at the opposite corner.

With the combined impacts of Clint's shoulder and his bullet, the sign gave way and dropped from the front of the building. Clint heard a short scream from Mackie before the weathered wooden planks fell onto him like judgment from above.

THIRTY-NINE

As much as Clint hated to admit it, he knew he wasn't going to catch up to Eli. Even though he checked the nearby roofs, Clint couldn't find any trace of him. The next thing he looked for was a way to get down from the roof he was on. Fortunately for him, Mackie wasn't going anywhere anytime soon.

Clint pulled open the trapdoor at the rear of the roof he was on and found himself looking down at a flat table full of folded blankets. Thankful that luck was on his side for a change, Clint dropped down into a fairly comfortable landing and hopped from the table.

"Pardon me, folks," he said to the nervous ladies inside the store. "I'll just be going now."

The store had a little bit of everything, but most of it was clothes. Apparently, almost half of the people in there had ducked in just to get off the street, because they were just as quick to duck right out again. Clint could see the fallen sign laying outside through the front widow. Since it was shifting up and down, he guessed there had to be someone underneath it.

After stepping out of the store, Clint drew his gun again and waited to see who might squirm out from beneath the cracked wooden sign. As soon as Mackie crawled out, Clint placed a foot on the sign and pressed it down on top of him a bit harder.

"Son of a bitch!" Mackie grunted.

Clint was quick to walk around to where Mackie was emerging from beneath the sign, so he could look down at the man's face as he placed his boot once more on the wooden corner. This time, he wasn't so quick to ease up.

"Sorry about that," Clint said. "Looks like you were in the wrong place at the wrong time."

Mackie wasn't surprised in the least to see Clint's face. In fact, he looked awfully close to spitting up at it. "Stand right there, Adams. My partner's about to put a bullet through your head any moment now."

"I think he'll have to run back another mile or so to get here," Clint replied. "He was in a pretty big hurry to get away the last I saw him."

"Just stay put and we'll find out."

"Why don't you throw out your gun while we wait?"

"I can't hardly move."

"Fine." With that, Clint raised his arm a bit, pointed the Colt at the sign, and pulled his trigger. His bullet punched a hole through the sign that wasn't anywhere close to Mackie's body, but nearly caused the man to jump out of his skin.

Mackie squirmed and shifted between the sign and the boardwalk. After one last twitch, a gun barrel poked out from beneath the fallen wood. "That's as good as I can do," he snarled.

"You can do a hell of a lot better if you tell me why those two Western Union men were killed."

"You gonna shoot me? Just do it. Otherwise, save yer fucking breath."

"John Blevin isn't anywhere near here," Clint said. "You've got to know that."

"What makes you think I give a shit about someone named Blevin?"

"If I find a sapphire on that gun of yours, I'll know you were one of the same group who tried to kill me and Johnny before."

Even though Mackie didn't say anything to that, he shifted his eyes toward his gun in a way that made Clint think he was on the right track.

Placing one foot flat on top of the sign, Clint stepped up onto it and walked across to the side where the barrel of Mackie's gun was sticking out. Every step he took was deliberately heavy, and each one brought a strained grunt from Mackie.

Clint hopped down and kicked the gun out from under the sign. Before he could reach for the discarded weapon, he caught a glimpse of movement coming from the otherwise deserted street. Even as Clint shifted to get a better look, part of him already knew what he would find.

Sure enough, by the time he spotted Eli, Clint was too late to get a shot off first before the other man's rifle fired.

Clint dropped down and felt the bullet crease his back. He rolled to one side, came up on one knee, and fired two quick shots at Eli.

The black man didn't even flinch. He knew he was outside of Clint's range, and didn't mind Clint wasting bullets. He also knew he wouldn't get many more clear shots, so he lined up the shot he knew he could hit and pulled his trigger.

The rifle cracked and hot lead drilled through the fallen sign. It also drilled a messy hole through the man trapped beneath it.

Without wasting another second, Eli turned tail and got the hell out of sight.

Clint's first impulse was to fire and cover himself as he moved to another spot, but when he saw Eli run away, he wanted to chase him. He jumped over the sign and ran a quarter of the way to the corner before realizing just how many turns Eli could have made in the time that had already passed.

Having seen firsthand how quickly Eli could run, Clint knew there wasn't a chance in hell for him to catch up now. Spitting out a frustrated curse through clenched teeth, Clint turned back around and walked toward the fallen sign.

Mackie was still under there, but he wasn't moving. By the time Clint knelt down and tried lifting the sign off of Mackie, he could tell the man was dying. The sign was heavy, but soon a few men had found their way out of a few different doorways to lend Clint a hand.

"You got anything to say to me?" Clint asked. "Or do you still want to protect the man who just sent you to your grave?"

Coughing up a mouthful of blood, Mackie grunted, "Go to . . . hell." His eyes were still fixed on Clint as the life in them dwindled away.

The locals who'd ventured onto the street flooded Clint with one question after another. Theirs and Clint's combined efforts were enough to lift the sign and drop it onto the street. Clint looked down at Mackie's body. His eyes were then drawn to the gun laying beside it.

FORTY

The lawman who ran down the street wasn't the same one Clint had spoken to before. He was a bit older and heavier. The badge on his chest marked him as a sheriff, but he carried himself in the same lackadaisical manner as his deputy. In fact, he approached the mess in the street as if he were looking at an overturned wagon instead of a dead body.

"Looks like we got us a mess," the sheriff said.

"Well," Clint snapped, "at least I can see you're not blind on top of being slow."

"No need for taking that tone, mister. You want to tell me what happened?"

"Sure. Should I start with me getting shot at or should I tell you about the assassin I chased out of here while you were off twiddling your thumbs somewhere?"

The sheriff looked angry, but he wasn't too quick to come to his own defense with a street full of locals glaring at him. "In case you didn't know, I have been trying to track down the killer of two men."

"I do know," Clint said. "I talked to one of your deputies about that."

"Save yer breath," one of the locals said. "He don't give

161

a damn unless you work for the railroad or Western Union. The rest of us don't pad his pockets enough to warrant any of his precious time."

"That's not true," the sheriff said.

"The hell it ain't!" another local said.

After that, the air was filled with more voices shouting so many words at the sheriff that they all blended together into a mush. What was easy enough to decipher was the fact that none of them were too happy about how the sheriff was doing his job.

"Everybody settle down," the sheriff said as he walked over to Clint. "Give me some room to move and I'll see what there is to see here." When he was next to Clint, he added, "And you can stop riling these folks up before I haul you into jail for inciting a riot."

"Are you kidding me?" Clint asked in disbelief.

Rather than try to back up the shallow threat he'd made, the sheriff squatted down to get a better look at Mackie. "You kill this man?" he asked.

"Actually, no," Clint said. "I dropped the sign on him, but didn't fire the shot that did him in."

"That dead man shot first!" one of the louder locals said. "You let that man alone. He shot to defend himself!"

"Is that true?" the sheriff asked.

Clint let out a sigh, knowing all too well where this was headed. "Yes, sir."

"Do you know why he took a shot at you?"

"Take a look at that gun."

The sheriff did and let out a low whistle. Mackie's gun lay right where its owner had dropped it. Although it wasn't as ornate as Franco's pistol, the plating had a fair amount of engraving, with a few small sapphires embedded where Mackie's fingers would have been when he was holding the grip. "Looks expensive."

"It also looks like the gun used by an assassin who tried to kill me and Johnny Blevin."

"Johnny's dead?"

The lawman's question brought a few shocked gasps from the locals who'd gathered around. Whispers immediately started flowing in the crowd.

"No," Clint said clearly enough for all to hear.

"And neither are you, I see," the sheriff added. "That means this assassin of yours ain't much of a killer. If it's all the same to you, I'll worry about the real deaths in my jurisdiction."

"I thought the Pinkertons were the ones who worried about that," Clint said.

"Whether it's me or the Pinkertons," the sheriff replied, "it ain't you who should be concerned about legal affairs. There's enough folks here vouching for you to keep you out of jail, but don't push me any farther. You understand?"

"Yeah."

"And don't leave town." The sheriff straightened up and held out his hand. "I'll have that gun of yours."

Clint could feel the blood running hot through his whole body. As much as he wanted to say to that sheriff, Clint settled for picking up the sapphire gun and slapping it into the lawman's hand. "Here. Take this gun instead. You'll probably be seeing another one like it soon enough."

With that, Clint turned his back to the entire scene and walked away.

Between the dead body on the ground and all the angry locals gathered around it, the sheriff had more problems to worry about than chasing after Clint.

FORTY-ONE

When Johnny had lived in his house, it was alive and kicking. When Clint had responded to Johnny's invitation, the house had been busting at the seams with rowdy drunks, willing women, and lively music. When Clint had returned after that, it was a quiet nesting place for a few scavenging killers.

Now the place felt like a ghost town.

Not only was the fence still broken, but even less of it was standing. Practically all the windows were shattered, and bodies lay strewn in the dirt. When Clint walked the property, he felt like he was trampling someone's poorly kept grave.

It didn't take long to survey the place. He rode around and could only find a few hungry critters darting for cover. Even Eclipse kept his head low, as if paying his respects to the dead and departed.

Clint swung down from the saddle so he could walk through the house. Despite the fact that he could practically see through the building from one window to another, he went inside and checked to be certain.

There was nobody scrounging around inside.

There was nobody hiding in the shadows.

There was just plain nobody.

Clint took a quick walk through the barn and was heading back to Eclipse when he saw another person on horseback coming up the trail. Before he even got a look at who it was, Clint drew the modified Colt and held it at the ready.

Judging by the wary smile on Victoria's face, she hadn't yet seen the gun in Clint's hand. "Is that you, Clint?" she asked.

Clint holstered the Colt and stood with Eclipse's reins in his hand. His other hand reached out to scratch the Darley Arabian's neck. "It's me."

She rode up to him and looked around. Soon, she was shaking her head. "This place looks awful."

"I know."

"John wouldn't like this one bit. He used to talk about how he was going to build this place up. I wonder what happened."

"I wouldn't worry about him," Clint said with a chuckle. "From what I hear, he made out just fine."

"That's right. Western Union bought him out. It all happened so quick I barely even noticed. I don't have much use for sending telegrams."

"Nothing wrong with that. Keep it simple and there's less to go wrong."

"You say that like you know all about it."

"Sometimes it feels like that's all I know."

She climbed down from her saddle and walked over to Clint. Her arms stretched out, and she slipped her fingers through his hair as if she somehow knew that would make him feel better. She couldn't have been more right.

"I heard about what happened in town," she said. "Sheriff Snetski isn't keeping you here. You could just leave and forget this place ever existed."

"That sounds like a dismissal."

Victoria's fingers stopped moving so she could pull

Clint's face closer to her own. "Not even close and you know it. You just look miserable and things around here are downright bleak. Folks have been screaming for Snetski to be replaced, but nobody's willing to take the badge for themselves. Now that the Western Union finally got what they wanted, they'll probably keep his dead ass right where it is."

"His name's Snetski?" Clint asked.

"Yep."

Nodding, he said, "He seems like a Snetski."

Victoria laughed, less at the joke and more at the lighter tone in Clint's voice. "He does, doesn't he?"

"What's Western Union see in him?"

"They probably like how well he fills out his chair rather than looking into anyone else's business. Don't all companies like that sort of thing in a sheriff?"

"I suppose so," Clint said. "You seem to know a lot about this sort of thing."

She shrugged and looked over to the broken-down, empty house. "Lots of people around here have been talking about it. I doubt even Johnny knew his deal was pretty much the talk of the town. The only thing folks were guessing about was how rich he got in the deal."

"Are they upset he sold?"

"Nobody blames him. Some may be a little jealous, but there's no hard feelings."

"That's nice to hear."

"It wasn't so nice to hear about those men shooting at you earlier," Victoria said with a shudder. "I was scared to death you were hurt." Suddenly, she pulled in a breath and turned Clint around. "Dear Lord, you are hurt!"

"What?" Only when he turned at the waist to try and see what she was talking about did Clint feel the burn from where the bullet had creased his back. "I almost forgot about that."

"Hasn't anyone looked at this?"

"Not yet."

"I'm taking you to the doctor."

"Would you mind bandaging me up?" Clint asked.

"I wouldn't mind."

"Then there's no need for a doctor."

"Don't be stubborn. Let's at least get somewhere clean."

Clint dug around in his saddlebags to find a roll of bandages and his canteen. "I'd rather stay here."

"Why? There's nothing here, and something over there looks like a dead body."

Rather than tell her that's exactly what it was, Clint said, "If there's any more of those assassins left, they'll probably be coming back here. It's the only spot where they might find a hint as to where Johnny went."

"Did he leave anything like a letter or such?"

"I don't think so, but an assassin wouldn't know that. Right about now, they'd be getting desperate for anything they could find."

"Like Johnny's friend who rode with him out of town?" Victoria asked sternly. "If they're after information about Johnny, you're the best source of it around here. Everyone knows that."

"I'm also the best chance he's got of getting to where he needs to go without someone tracking him down and putting a bullet in him. So long as they keep coming after me, there aren't as many going after him. There might not even be any who know where to look for him."

"You must be a good friend of his," she said.

Clint nodded a bit and then shrugged. "He's a good guy and I told him I'd watch his back. I also don't like the thought of a bunch of assholes shooting their guns like they've got nobody to answer to, especially when they shoot at me."

"If the assassins are here, or if there's any left alive, isn't Johnny already far away from them?"

"These seem to be more than just hired guns. They're

more organized. They just might be able to send someone
out to another state with a telegram placed at the right time
or a signal passed to the right person."

"Don't you think they would have been to this house
already?"

Glancing over at the body laying not too far away, Clint
said, "Probably."

"Then if these killers are so smart, why would they
come back?"

Clint thought for a few seconds, but was unable to come
up with a good answer. The best he could do was "Good
point."

FORTY-TWO

"How's the new room?" the man behind the desk asked.

Clint was walking through the hotel lobby carrying a small bundle of ham sandwiches he'd gotten from the place's kitchen. Compared with how he'd started his day, he was a new man. His wound was cleaned and bandaged. He'd stretched out and rested his eyes for a bit. He was even feeling good enough to smile back at the clerk when he said, "Just fine. Any problem with our arrangement?"

"Not at all. You sure we can't convince you to run for sheriff?"

Laughing, Clint walked to the stairs that led to the second floor. "I'll think it over."

"You do that! Oh, and don't forget this. It was just brought over."

Clint walked back to the desk and took the folded paper the clerk was holding out to him. He got it open, saw the letterhead, and asked, "This is a telegram and it just arrived? Isn't the Western Union office closed by now?"

"It is, but they sent a runner out to make deliveries before it got too late. Things are kind of a mess over at that office."

"Yeah, I suppose they are." After reading more of what was written on the paper, Clint grinned.

"Nothing bad, I hope," the clerk said.

"Not at all. Thanks."

When Clint got to his room and opened the door, he found Victoria waiting there for him. She was dressed in a thin white slip, and she immediately rushed over to take the sandwiches from him.

"Where have you been?" she asked.

"Look at what's in your hands. That should answer your question."

"You were just supposed to get some water. Actually, you weren't supposed to even do that."

"Relax. This cut on my back isn't anything worth all this fuss."

"It's more than just a cut," she muttered. Still, even she couldn't justify saying much more since she'd been the one to clean up the crease on Clint's back and wrap it in bandages. The bullet had torn a bloody gash down his body, but it was only a nasty-looking flesh wound.

"Someone's bringing the water," Clint said. "And along the way, I got hungry. I got something for you, too."

That brightened Victoria's face a bit. "Really? What did you get me?"

"Ham sandwiches. It's all they had left in the kitchen. They offered to toss a steak on the fire, but I wouldn't let them go through the trouble."

Victoria laughed and unwrapped the sandwiches. "Folks around here really want you to stay. You'd make a fine sheriff." Looking up at him, she added, "And it wouldn't be too hard. This place hasn't seen so much gunfire since . . . well . . . ever."

"All the excitement's just riled everyone up."

"That and Sheriff Snetski is looking to hire himself out to anyone willing to pay."

Clint took a sandwich, bit into it, and winced. "I don't

know if there's any real reason Western Union would want
to buy a crooked sheriff. They do just fine on their own.
Besides, when push came to shove they hired the Pinkertons to represent their interests."

Victoria's eyes shot open and she jumped up from
where she'd been sitting on the edge of the bed. "Oh! I almost forgot to tell you. The Pinkerton man's here. He arrived while you were sleeping."

"I was only resting my eyes."

"I guess you always snore like that when you rest your
eyes," she said to chide him. "Anyway, the sheriff's been
showing a stranger around to where that sign fell down and
that man was shot. He's dressed in a nice suit and everyone's
been saying he's a Pinkerton. You want to go see him?"

"Eh, if he wants to talk to me, he should be able to find
me. That's what those Pinkertons do."

"You don't seem too worked up about it anymore."

"My part in this is done," Clint said plainly.

"And when did you decide that?"

"As soon as I read this." With a grin, Clint produced the
telegram that he'd been given at the front desk.

The telegram read:

> Am boarding the boat now
> Safe and sound
> Thanks for everything
>   JB

"What boat?" Victoria asked.

"Doesn't even matter. What does matter is that he's on
it, and if he didn't run into any assassins by now, he's out
of their reach."

"You're sure that's from him?"

Clint nodded. "He and I are the only ones knowing he
was headed for a boat. I hoped to draw enough fire for him
to get there safely and he's there. My job's done."

Frowning, Victoria asked, "So that means you'll be leaving soon?"

"Tomorrow."

"Well then, I guess we should make the best out of what time we have left." As she said that, Victoria took the sandwich from Clint's hand and tossed it onto a nearby table. She unbuttoned her blouse and reached for the lantern on the wall.

As the light faded away, Clint could feel her pulling him closer to the bed. His eyes weren't adjusted to the dark just yet, but he could hear the rustle of her clothes being pulled off. Soon, he could feel the tug of her hands on his belt. Just as his jeans were being pulled down, there was a knock on the door.

"That's probably our water," he said.

"If we're quiet, they'll just leave it."

Clint was more than willing to do just that, but he waited until he actually heard the sound of something being set in the hall just outside the door and the receding footsteps that followed. Opening the door a crack, Clint saw the pitcher of water as well as the maid who was already heading for the stairs.

"All right," Clint said as he closed the door, locked it, and turned toward the bed. "Where were we?"

FORTY-THREE

Even after he'd adjusted to the dark, Clint still couldn't see much more than shapes amid the shadows. The curtains were drawn. The moon was barely a sliver outside. There wasn't even enough light trickling in from the cracks in the doorway to be of any use.

But Clint didn't need to see anything. His other senses had more than enough to keep him busy. He could smell the scent of Victoria's skin and hair as she undressed him and pulled him down onto the bed. He could feel the smooth texture of her breasts and belly as he moved his hands along the front of her body.

His fingers drifted through the downy patch of hair between her legs, and soon he could taste the tender lips of her pussy. He heard her moan and then call his name urgently.

"Come up here, Clint," she whispered. "I want you inside of me."

Clint climbed onto the bed and felt her legs open and then wrap around him. His cock was already rigid, and the moment he felt it brush against her damp pussy, it got even harder. Victoria's fingers gently closed around his shaft and guided him into her. With one push, he was in, and he slid all the way until he completely filled her.

She made a contented sound that was close to a purr, and her fingernails scraped across Clint's shoulders. He pumped in and out of her, taking a slow, easy rhythm so he could savor every last moment. Propping himself on one elbow, Clint used his other hand to fondle her breasts. He teased her nipples until she began writhing beneath him.

"What was that?" she whispered.

Clint's thumb was drawing a line between her breasts when he said, "I thought you liked that."

"Not that. I mean the sound. Did you hear it?"

Clint stopped what he was doing and listened.

"It sounds like it's coming from the old room."

"Yeah," Clint replied. "That's what I'm thinking."

Upon his return, Clint had asked to be moved into the room next to the one he'd had before. The manager at the front desk had been perfectly happy to fill the request and even filled Clint's second request, which was to keep the old room written in the ledger.

In a matter of seconds, Clint was up, dressed, and had his Colt in hand. "Stay here," he said. "I'll be right back."

In the darkness, Clint was just able to see Victoria nodding.

Clint opened the door gently so as not to make a sound. He tiptoed to the neighboring door, saw it was slightly ajar, and placed his free hand flat against it just above the handle. Once he'd steeled himself, Clint pushed the door open and jumped inside.

Crouching between the bed and the window, Eli snapped his head around in surprise. He also had a gun in hand, but he didn't move right away.

For the space of a few heartbeats, both men stood where they were and stared at each other.

Clint had switched rooms to guard against this very thing.

Eli had gone from setting a trap to springing one in the blink of an eye.

Now both men had to decide what they were going to do about it.

FORTY-FOUR

Eli was the first to move. He fired a quick shot while turning toward the window and then used his gun to smash out the glass.

The room filled with the thunder of that shot, but the bullet buried itself in the wall well away from where Clint was standing.

"Oh no you don't," Clint said as he launched himself through the air and over the bed. Clint's stomach slammed against the mattress and his left hand clenched around Eli's belt.

Although Eli's forward momentum carried Clint a little ways across the bed, it wasn't enough to get him out the window. Clint pulled his arm back and dragged Eli away from the window, until the black man knocked against the small table beside the bed.

Clint swung his legs over the mattress and jumped onto the floor. Eli brought his pistol around to aim at Clint's head, but Clint grabbed the man's gun hand and forced it toward the ceiling. Eli's pistol barked once more and put a hole over their heads. As he felt Eli's grip tightening again around the pistol's grip, Clint forced his arm in another direction.

Eli gritted his teeth and struggled to get away from Clint. He was simply out-manned, which was why he'd tried to run in the first place. Clint outweighed Eli by at least fifty pounds, and a lot of that was muscle. It wasn't easy, but Clint was able to force Eli's arm down toward the broken window.

When he felt the first touch of broken glass against his arm, Eli turned to look at what Clint was doing. He saw his arm lowering onto a jagged shard of glass. That put some more urgency into Eli's efforts, which got him to raise his arm a bit. That burst of strength didn't last long before Clint leaned in and muscled through it.

The glass sliced into Eli's arm like a hot knife through butter. Clint tightened his grip and pushed down a bit more, until he felt Eli's grip loosen. As soon as the gun dropped from Eli's hand, Clint pulled his arm off the glass and threw Eli to the corner of the room.

With the pain flooding through his arm, and the exertion of the struggle taking hold, Eli didn't do much more than slouch against the wall. He grabbed the sheets off the bed and pressed them to his arm. "I was gonna run," Eli said. "I wasn't gonna shoot you."

"That's only because you knew you wouldn't walk out of here alive if you did."

Eli shook his head weakly. "I could've shot you in the street, but I didn't."

"Why not?" Clint asked.

Now that he'd caught his breath, Eli looked up at Clint and showed him a tired smile. "I signed on with them killers just to get out of jail. I did what I had to do until I got a chance to be rid of 'em."

"What about now?"

"Now . . . jail's looking pretty good."

Clint lifted Eli to his feet and used the sheets to tie his wrists together behind his back. When he stepped into the hallway with Eli in tow, Clint leaned toward his new room and found Victoria peeking through the cracked-open door. He told her, "I'm all right. I'll be right back."

Once downstairs, Clint saw the manager of the hotel rushing out to meet him. "I sent for the—" was all he got out before the front door swung open.

The sheriff stomped inside, and another man wearing a dark suit was following him. "What's going on here?" the sheriff asked. "Was there shots fired?"

"Yes, sir," Clint replied. "And here's the man who fired them." With that, Clint shoved Eli toward the lawman.

The man in the suit practically shoved the sheriff aside. "Does this man know about the assassins who killed the Western Union men?"

"Oh yes," Clint said.

"Then I'll take him."

Clint handed Eli over gratefully. "He's all yours."

"Your name?"

"Clint Adams."

The man in the suit nodded. "I've heard a lot about you. David Roper. I'm with the Pinkerton Agency."

"I suppose you'll want to drag me over the coals with some more questions?"

Roper shook his head. "I've heard so much about you, I'm sick of you." Grinning, he added, "Everyone in town said you weren't doing anything but trying to help around here. Every shot you fired was in self-defense and you can do no wrong. I'd appreciate it if you stopped by to fill me in, but it can wait until morning."

"No problem."

"Once I verify the identity of these killers, you'll probably have a reward coming to you," Roper continued. "They've got a hell of a price on their heads, and Western Union is paying it."

That wasn't much of a surprise to Clint. Even though Galloway had been one of the men to hire the sapphire guns, it only made sense that Galloway's superiors would pay to have the witnesses to the botched assassinations captured as soon as possible. For the moment, Clint just wanted to put the whole thing behind him.

"I'd shake your hand, Adams," Roper said, "but mine are full right now. Why don't I buy you breakfast tomorrow and I can get you that reward? Some of my men will stay here just in case any more of these killers gives you any grief."

Clint was already heading back up the stairs. "I appreciate the thought," he said. "But I think these fellows have had enough."

FORTY-FIVE

Clint opened the door and stepped into his room. He could see Victoria laying under the covers, so he closed the door behind him and stripped out of his clothes.

"No need to worry," he said. "It was just one last try before the cavalry arrived. The Pinkertons are downstairs, so I figure I'll let them sweep up whatever's left so they don't feel like they wasted a trip."

Laying down, Clint felt like a weight had been lifted from his shoulders. He was also exhausted after carrying that weight for the last few days. He felt Victoria's hands rubbing his chest and didn't make a move.

"I could use some sleep," he said. "Why don't I wake you up later?"

Her answer to that was to throw the covers aside and crawl on top of him. Her nails clawed into his chest and she was breathing heavily as she leaned forward to lick his neck.

"I guess that got your blood going, huh?"

"Just glad you're safe," she whispered.

Clint paused, but before he could say anything, he felt her soft pussy grinding against his cock. She kept rubbing against him until he was hard, and the way her hips were moving, that didn't take long. Finally, she reached down to take his penis in her hand.

"Victoria? What's wrong?"

The muscles in her legs were taut against his thighs. She guided him into her and slid all the way down his cock. Clint strained his eyes, but could only see the shape of her moving above him. It didn't help matters that he'd just come in from the much better lit hallway.

Victoria straightened up and ground her hips against Clint's. She rode his cock like she'd been craving it for weeks, and started letting out a series of throaty moans.

As good as she was making him feel, Clint knew something was wrong. Forcing himself to think clearly just then was like trying to read a newspaper through a thick fog. Then, Clint gave in and focused completely on what he'd been trying to ignore.

He concentrated on how her body rocked on top of him and how it felt to slide in and out of her.

Clint pulled in a breath and let the scent of Victoria's hair flow through him.

And then he knew what was wrong.

That wasn't Victoria.

Just as Clint put that together, he felt one of the woman's hands leave his chest. It was at that same moment that he knew who she was.

"I wish I could see your face right now," Rosa hissed. "I'll bet you look so surprised."

Reflexively, Clint reached out for her hands. One was still on his chest and he grabbed it at the wrist. When he reached for the other, he managed to knock it away as it swung toward him. Clint felt cold steel graze the palm of his hand, and he knew Rosa was holding a knife.

"I'll have plenty of time to see you when you're dead," she snarled.

Clint waited until he felt her shift her weight forward. Once it did, he swung his arm in a wide, powerful arc that caught Rosa's elbow. She writhed on top of him, still grinding her hips as if she was about to climax while in the middle of the fight.

While their arms were tangled together, Clint got his fingers around her wrist and just got ahold of her when Rosa's blade brushed against his cheek. Even now that he had a hold on her wrist, it still wasn't easy to push her back.

She leaned forward, shifting all of her weight behind her thin knife. The sapphire in the handle glittered like a single star in the shadowy room. "I'll bet you never suspected me of anything, Clint. You're like every other man. Thinking with your dick, and not enough balls to stand up to a woman."

"Of course I suspected you," Clint said as he pushed the blade an inch or so back. "In case you don't remember, you never did get out of those ropes."

"Yeah, but you had no clue I was the one setting up all the deals and handling all those jobs."

"I guessed it might be you. That whole sapphire thing could only be a woman's idea."

Just then, the lantern blazed to life and filled the room with a rich glow.

Clint could see Rosa on top of him. She was naked and sweating with the exertion of the fight. She also held a slender knife in her hand that looked more like a sliver of steel.

Victoria had been the one to turn the knob on the lantern. Rosa turned to get a look at her, which gave Clint a chance to make one more push. That was all he needed to twist Rosa's wrist and force her to drop the knife. His other hand went to her throat as he sat upright in bed.

"What . . . now?" Rosa croaked through the grip Clint had on her throat. "You die . . . or I do."

Clint sat there with her life in his hands. He started to squeeze, but couldn't help from feeling the pang of guilt for strangling a helpless, naked woman. The same instincts that had saved his life before now caused his fingers to loosen.

The second Rosa felt his fingers let go, she smiled and pulled free of his hand. She started to dive for her knife, but couldn't find it on the floor.

That was because it was no longer on the floor.

The knife was in Victoria's hand and she buried that blade deep into Rosa's shoulder.

Rosa turned and showed a savage mix of pain and rage in her eyes. Victoria pulled the knife out, balled up her other hand, and punched Rosa square in the jaw. Finally, Rosa dropped. She landed half on the bed, with her arms and head dangling over the side.

Pulling Rosa all the way up, Clint jumped off the bed and picked up his gun. Before the Colt was securely in his grasp, Victoria rushed over to him.

She dropped the knife so she could wrap both arms around Clint. After hugging him, she looked up at him. There was a fresh bruise on her face and some blood in her hair running from a cut on her scalp. "She came in while you were downstairs. She . . . tried to knock me out, but . . ."

"It's all right," Clint said. "Are you hurt too badly?"

Reluctantly, she shook her head. "I feel better now that I paid her back for bushwhacking me."

Clint laughed and held her close. "Maybe you should run for sheriff."

Watch for

ONE MAN'S LAW

306th novel in the exciting GUNSMITH series
from Jove

Coming in June!

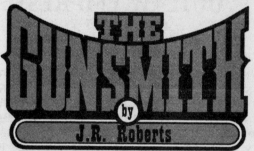

GIANT-SIZED ADVENTURE FROM
AVENGING ANGEL LONGARM.

LONGARM AND THE
OUTLAW EMPRESS
0-515-14235-2

WHEN DEPUTY U.S. MARSHAL CUSTIS LONG STOPS
A STAGECOACH ROBBERY, HE TRACKS THE BANDITS
TO A TOWN CALLED ZAMORA. A HAVEN FOR
THE LAWLESS, IT'S RULED BY ONE OF THE MOST
POWERFUL, BRILLIANT, AND BEAUTIFUL WOMEN
IN THE WEST...A WOMAN WHOM LONGARM WILL
HAVE TO FACE, UP CLOSE AND PERSONAL.

Giant Westerns featuring
The Gunsmith

LITTLE SURESHOT AND THE
WILD WEST SHOW
0-515-13851-7

DEAD WEIGHT
0-515-14028-7

RED MOUNTAIN
0-515-14206-9